JODI:

The Secret in the Silver Box

Virginia Work

*Best wishes from your
Sunday School teachers,
Janet Uhlinger and
Esther Ebersole*

MOODY PRESS
CHICAGO

Library of Congress Cataloging in Publication Data

Work, Virginia, 1946-
  Jodi: the secret in the silver box.

  SUMMARY: A young Christian, vacationing near an old
Canadian mining town, helps an elderly prospector solve the
mystery of a silver box before it falls into the wrong hands.
  [1. Mystery and detective stories. 2. Christian life—Fiction.
3. Canada—Fiction]. I. Title.

PZ7.W8875Jo   [Fic]   80-11987

ISBN 0-8024-4417-2

Moody Press, a ministry of the Moody Bible Institute, is
designed for education, evangelization, and edification.
If we may assist you in knowing more about Christ and
the Christian life, please write us without obligation:
Moody Press, c/o MLM, Chicago, Illinois 60610.

Printed in the United States of America

Contents

To my husband, Dan,
and to my three children,
Brian, Sherry, and
Vickie

1

An Old Prospector

In the middle of the narrow street, Jodi Fischer paused and glanced around uneasily. She squinted her pretty blue eyes against the hot afternoon sun and ran her fingers through her short, reddish brown curls.

"Now, where *is* that dog?" she whispered to herself. She had already gone far past the last of the restored buildings in the old ghost town of Barkerville, searching for her white terrier puppy, Sugar.

"I thought I saw her come this way," she muttered under her breath. She shifted from one foot to another and peered into the woods and on down the road. The old gold rush town in central British Columbia lay quiet and brooding over its sins in the past. A spooky feeling crept up Jodi's back.

She shook herself, and then to her left, she heard a dog bark. It was Sugar! She glanced around quickly and noticed a tiny road leading into the woods.

"Sugar!" Her voice croaked and she trotted down the narrow road, her heart pounding. "Oh, I hope she isn't far. Wonder what's down this road. I hope nobody's ghost—" She turned a corner in the road and stopped, staring straight ahead.

There was a small clearing, and a log cabin with a blue Volkswagen parked in front of it. But what she was staring at was the old man sitting on the steps in front of the cabin.

He was an old-timer, his floppy, wide-brimmed hat pulled low over his forehead, and his face brown and wrinkled. He was patting a fluffy little white dog.

"Sugar! Come here!" Jodi called. The little dog ran to her, and she leaned over and picked her up.

The old man stood up nimbly and walked to Jodi.

5

He was not much taller than she, and he wore patched jeans held up by suspenders, with a red plaid shirt. He smelled of tobacco and sweat, and there was a stubble of beard on his chin.

"Nice pup," he said. His blue eyes sparkled with fun, and a smile creased his face.

Jodi grinned. "Thanks. She's always running away, though. Sorry to bother you." She began edging away.

The man chuckled. It was a comfortable, happy sound. "Oh, no bother. I'm kinda lonesome back in here. Not every day a cute pup and a pretty girl come callin'." He said it so sincerely that Jodi did not feel embarrassed.

"Are—are you a prospector, sir?" she asked, her blue eyes widening.

"Call me Joe, miss," he said with another chuckle. "Most folks call me Sucker Joe, cuz I never did strike it rich." He turned and walked back to the cabin. "Come on up and chat a spell," he said.

He climbed the steps and settled in a wicker chair on the porch. Jodi perched on the top step and let Sugar down.

"Come up here every summer and pan a little gold from the crick," Joe went on. "Never find much, but you never know." He dug in his pockets and pulled out a little tin box and a paper. He tapped the box to let a small amount of brown stuff fall onto the paper. Then he glanced at Jodi and ducked his head.

"Don't mind if I smoke, do you?" he asked.

She shook her head, and watched as he expertly rolled the paper around the tobacco, licked the end of it, lit a match, and then leaned back to enjoy his smoke.

"My pappy built this here cabin," he said proudly. "Durin' the gold rush days. He and my uncle struck it rich on the crick just over there a ways." He motioned vaguely through the woods. "And what is your name?"

"Jodi," she answered. "Jodi Fischer. We live down by Richburg. My parents are missionaries to the Indian people. We came with my best friend, MaryAnn, and her dad to see Barkerville, and then we're going to camp out at Bowron Lakes for the rest of the week." She paused and then grinned. "But I never thought I'd meet a real, live prospector!"

She half expected the jolly laugh once more, but Joe's eyes dropped and his shoulders slumped.

"No, miss," he said with a sigh. "I ain't really no prospector. A prospector could live on what he found, but I cain't. I've tried all my life to be as good as my pappy, and give my money to some fine charity, but I just cain't. I guess I'm no good." He sighed again.

For a minute, Jodi did not know what to say. She had often felt the pain of failure and the awful conviction that she was not worth much. So she swallowed and smiled a little.

"That's not true," she said. "I'm sure you've tried your hardest, and you seem like a real nice person to me."

Joe straightened up, studied Jodi's face for a second, and then leaned back in his chair. A worried expression still haunted his eyes.

"There might be a way," he said softly, almost to himself, studying the tops of the trees. "If only I could find—" He paused and looked piercingly at Jodi. "I need help. I don't suppose you would—"

She nodded. "I'll do anything I can, Joe, that is, if—if it's not against the law."

Joe smiled, hope leaping into his eyes. "Against the law? No, this is all right that way. You see—" He leaned forward and lowered his voice. "I was goin' through some of Pappy's things again in the back room, and I found a letter I'd never seen before. It musta been written just afore he died. In it, he said he wanted me to have a silver box that was given to him by a Chinese man for saving his life."

"Chinese?" Jodi asked.

Joe nodded. "Used to be lots of 'em here at Barkerville. They were good at plantin' gardens and sellin' stuff to the miners. Well, this one was gittin' robbed when my pappy happened by and chased them crooks out of there. And this man, he gives Pappy some money and also this silver box." He paused. "I remember that box—it was made out of real silver, and on the top a dragon was engraved, and the dragon had two little emeralds for eyes."

"Real ones?"

"Yup. But I haven't seen that box for a long time. Pappy musta hid it somewheres. I've been lookin' all over the cabin for it, but I cain't find it. The only place left is the attic." Joe stood up and led the way to a small, high window at the back of the cabin.

"It's really just a small crawl space," Joe said, his voice still low. "But I don't want to go up no ladder, and I wouldn't fit through that window, neither."

Jodi swallowed. She looked up at the window and back at Joe. "You—you mean, you want me to go up there and look around for that silver box?"

Joe nodded. Suddenly a twig snapped in the woods, and Sugar started barking and running toward the sound. Jodi ran to catch her.

"Sugar! Come here!" She grabbed the dog as she tried to dodge past her legs. "Bad dog! You can't chase every squirrel in the woods!" Jodi hung onto her collar and trotted back to the cabin.

The old man had leaned a ladder against the cabin, and now he turned to Jodi. His face was pale, and there was fear in his eyes.

"Now!" he whispered. "You have to go now. Hurry! Please!" He wiped his sweaty forehead with the back of his hand.

Jodi hesitated for a second and then scrambled up the ladder, crawled through the opening, and found herself in a tiny room the length of the cabin. The roof slanted so close to her head that she could not stand up. The room was filled with old, dusty wooden crates, all kinds of rusty tools, and piles of yellowed papers and magazines. It smelled dank and dusty.

"Oh, yuk," Jodi mumbled to herself. "How do I get into things like this? I'm just dumb enough—" She went on mumbling to herself, lifting the tops of the boxes, picking up piles of papers, and moving the tools to look behind them.

She was on the far side of the cabin, near the front, when she heard Sugar barking again. Then she heard a funny scraping noise alongside the cabin. She began crawling back to the window, but her progress was slow. And then, it seemed just below her feet, she could hear the voices of men talking. She could not hear the words, but it seemed one was talking in a bossy way. There was a scuffle, then footsteps going out of the cabin. She listened for a little longer, but all was quiet.

She reached the window and looked out. The ladder was gone! Her fingernails dug into the wood on the windowsill, and she felt dizzy. *What is going on here?* The question whirled in her mind and her heart beat hard.

"Joe!" she called, but no one came, and her voice echoed off the trees. Sugar came panting around the corner of the house and looked up at her, wagging her short tail.

"Oh, Sugar!" she said, relieved to see her. "You're not much help, but I'm glad you didn't run off again." She sat back on her heels and tried to think. *What should I do? Maybe there's a piece of old rope up here, or something else I can let myself down with.*

She crawled back into the attic and rummaged through the piles of dusty tools and papers.

"Here's something!" she exclaimed, lifting up a length of rusty chain. "Not very long, but then this window isn't too high, either."

Near the windowsill she found a nail sticking out. She looped the last link of the chain over that, tested it, and then wiggled out the window, feet first. With her toes she

9

felt for a crack between the logs and slowly worked herself out the window and down the side of the cabin, holding onto the chain.

"Ugh!" she grunted, resting for a moment. The chain bit into her hands and her arms were tiring. "If only—I had—long legs like MaryAnn," she muttered. She glanced down and saw the ground fairly close, so she kicked out from the cabin and let go of the chain. She hit the ground hard, skinning her elbow and twisting her ankle.

"Oh, oh, that hurts!" She moaned, rocking back and forth on the ground. Sugar came up and licked her face. Jodi rubbed her ankle and then stood up carefully, testing her weight on it.

"Hm, doesn't seem too bad," she said, brushing the dirt from her legs and shorts. Then she picked up Sugar. "C'mon, girl, I'm going to put you in the Laine's motor home, and then MaryAnn and I are coming back to find that box!"

Barkerville was teeming with life on the long, hot walk back to the picnic area near the lot where Mr. Laine had parked the motor home. Jodi dodged the tourists and gazed at the tall buildings, the boardwalks, the old church at the end of the street, and the huge waterwheel near the museum. She could hear the horse-drawn stagecoach coming down the street and the clink of metal as people tried their luck at the gold-panning attraction.

She found MaryAnn outside the motor home looking, as usual, cool and fresh. Her long, dark hair was brushed neatly down her back, and her big, brown eyes were calm.

"You look hot!" MaryAnn exclaimed as she unlocked the door.

Jodi sighed. "I am!" She put Sugar inside, and then the two of them walked to the refreshment stand where MaryAnn bought two ice cream cones. Brian, Jodi's ten-year-old brother, was just finishing a tall Coke, his blond hair falling into his eyes.

"Where have you been?" MaryAnn asked, glancing at Jodi's smudged shorts. "Up to something exciting, I bet."

Jodi's long, dark lashes veiled her eyes for a moment while she licked her ice cream. Brian sauntered off to watch the stagecoach go by. Jodi leaned closer to Mary-Ann.

"It's more than exciting," she said. "It's a—" and here she lowered her voice to a whisper, "mystery!"

MaryAnn's brown eyes flickered with excitement for a moment, and then she chuckled. "Oh, Jodi. I think the atmosphere of this old town has gotten to you." She sighed elaborately. "But I suppose I'll have to humor you and get in on this mystery of yours." Her voice was loaded with sarcasm, but Jodi knew she was only teasing. They began walking down the crowded street, eyeing the horses that were pulling the stagecoach.

Jodi thought of her golden quarter horse, Honey, and the fun she and MaryAnn had had at the gymkhana last week. She and Honey had brought home a first place in the barrel racing.

Suddenly Jodi stopped. "Look!" she said. "There's Angel." She nodded her head toward a slim, attractive blonde girl coming down the street.

"Who?" MaryAnn asked.

"Angel. Angel Lewis. She's in my class at school. And look who's with her!" A tall, tanned boy with wavy brown hair was walking toward them, talking to Angel.

"Whew! He's cute," MaryAnn replied. "What's his name?"

Jodi edged back into the doorway of a restored dry goods store. "Ron Carson. He is really nice. Comes to Young People's once in a while. He has some horses, too."

"Looks like they make a good couple," MaryAnn ob-

11

served. Jodi flashed her an angry look. "They're not going steady. This is the first time I've seen them together. But, of course, Angel's got the looks to get whoever she wants." She pulled MaryAnn into the store as the two walked by.

"Why'd you do that?" MaryAnn asked her. "I wanted to meet him—I mean, them."

"Oh, I'd *die* if he saw me like this!" Jodi exclaimed, running her hand through her flyaway curls. "I'm so dirty and ugly. Anyway, next to Angel, I feel like a toad." She sighed as they walked outside again, and she glanced at Ron's retreating back. "Of course, he'd never look at me anyway, even if Angel weren't around."

MaryAnn shook her head angrily and her dark eyes snapped. "Jodi, sometimes you make me so mad! You really are pretty, you know, and I don't know anyone as creative as you!"

"Creative!" Jodi repeated sarcastically.

"Yes," MaryAnn replied. They walked around a group of people and looked at the figure of Billy Barker standing outside the hole where he had struck it rich. MaryAnn glanced at Jodi.

"I wish I could do half the stuff you can do," she said. "Like art, and the knack you have with writing stories, and decorating cakes, and a lot of other things, too. You're always thinking up neat ideas for Young People's."

Jodi shrugged. "Anyone can have ideas. I feel so— so dumb and tongue-tied, especially around boys. Most of the time I feel like a big, fat zero. In fact, that's what that man I met earlier said, too."

"What man?"

"The man who owns a cabin up here, and he's a real prospector, and he wanted me to find this silver box, so I—"

MaryAnn raised her hand. "Hey, wait a minute! Would you mind starting at the beginning?"

So Jodi told her all that had happened earlier, and

just as she finished, they rounded the turn and saw the old cabin.

They both paused. The cabin was larger than those in Barkerville, and it was built of sturdy logs. There was a small patch of grass in front, and even a tiny garden to one side. The blue Volkswagen seemed strangely out of place. It was deathly quiet.

MaryAnn gripped Jodi's arm. "The car's still there," she whispered. "But no one's around. Shall we go back?"

Jodi shook her head firmly. "No way. I want to find that silver box. Maybe something happened to Joe. He seemed really nervous." They entered the clearing slowly and approached the cabin.

Jodi's mouth was dry, but she clenched her teeth and walked up to the cabin. She knocked on the door, but there was no answer. By the side of the cabin, on the ground, was the ladder. She and MaryAnn raised it to the window.

MaryAnn pushed her hair back. "Don't tell me you're going to go in there again and leave me all alone out here," she whispered.

"You can come if you want to," Jodi whispered back. Then she looked at MaryAnn and grinned. "Why are we whispering?"

MaryAnn glanced around fearfully. "Because it's so scary!" she hissed. "Now, hurry!"

Jodi climbed the ladder once more, but instead of rummaging through the boxes, she sat on her heels and thought.

Now, if I were Joe's father, and I wanted to hide that box where it would be hard to find, where would I hide it? Not in those old boxes, that's for sure. And I wouldn't leave it out with the tools and magazines.

She began studying the logs that held up the roof. They were about ten inches thick and placed about eighteen inches apart, going vertically up to the peak.

"Maybe I'd hollow out a little space in one of those

logs," she muttered. Then she started to feel each log, from the far corner near the floor to the peak. That meant moving boxes and tools. By the time she reached the other end of the cabin, she was beginning to feel discouraged and tired. But then a piece of the log near the floor moved to her touch.

"Oh!" she exclaimed. "This must be it!" She felt breathless with excitement as she pulled a rough little door away from the log. Inside was a small, hollowed-out space.

And there, sitting neatly in the space, was a dullish gray silver box.

2

The Clue in the Silver Box

Jodi reached gingerly into the hole and drew out the box. It was small, maybe four inches wide and six inches long. The silver glinted even though it was tarnished.

"MaryAnn! I found it!" she called. She heard a muffled sound from below, and a few minutes later, MaryAnn's head appeared in the window.

"Bring it over here, Jodi," MaryAnn said breathlessly. "What is it like?"

Jodi crawled over to the window and held the box in the sunlight. "It's heavy," she said. "And, oh, look! Here's the dragon engraved on the lid of the box." She pulled out the tail of her blouse and dusted off the top.

"Oh, look at the eyes!" MaryAnn exclaimed. She touched the two tiny flashing eyes of the dragon. "Emeralds! Just think!"

"I wonder what's in it?" Jodi said and lifted the lid of the box. It was empty. "Nothing!" She sighed. "Oh, well, I can give Joe his silver box, anyway."

MaryAnn backed down the ladder, and Jodi followed her to the ground. MaryAnn glanced around.

"What do we do with it, now?" she asked uneasily. "We shouldn't leave something so valuable just lying around."

Jodi nodded. "I wish Joe were here. I wonder what's happened to him, and why he wanted this box so badly."

"Well, we can't leave it here, so I guess we'll have to take it back with us. C'mon, Jodi, this place gives me the creeps."

MaryAnn tucked her hair behind her ears and led the way out of the clearing. The sun was setting over the trees, and Jodi shivered. Just before they turned the

15

corner, she glanced back into the woods beyond the cabin.

"Oh!" she exclaimed, grabbing MaryAnn's arm. "I thought I saw someone just now—just out of the corner of my eye—coming out of those woods over there."

MaryAnn whirled around and studied the old cabin and the woods.

"Nothing there now," she whispered. "Are you going back?"

Jodi gulped. "No. But I wonder—who would be sneaking around like that?"

"I don't know." MaryAnn sighed. "But I'm not going to wait until they jump us from these bushes." They began walking swiftly down the narrow road and then through Barkerville.

They were going by the tall theater building when Jodi looked back again.

"There! I did see someone this time!" she said. "That small, thin man back there. I bet he's following us."

"Oh, it's just your imagination," MaryAnn said, glancing over her shoulder. But Jodi noticed her pace quickened until they were nearly running.

Past the fire hall with its tall water tower, the assay office, the dentist's, and the hairdresser's they hurried, Jodi clutching the little silver box.

"C'mon, back here!" she panted, pulling MaryAnn behind the Wake Up Jake Cafe.

"Is—is he still—back there?" MaryAnn panted, glancing back down the street as she followed Jodi.

Jodi shook her head. "I don't know. Saw him back there a ways." They ran behind several buildings and then came out at the gold-panning attraction. They mingled with the crowd and then walked the rest of the way to the motor home.

Jodi's mother was just setting an outside picnic table for dinner when Jodi and MaryAnn walked up. Sugar, who was tied to the table, barked a greeting.

"Oh, here you are," Mrs. Fischer said with a smile.

16

She was slim and attractive, her brown hair waving gently to her shoulders. Her blue eyes held a tinge of rebuke. "I was beginning to get worried."

"Hi, Mom," Jodi said. "We were just—ah, exploring." She stooped to pat Sugar and then followed MaryAnn into the motor home.

It was luxurious and sparkling new. Jodi would never have said the word *rich* to MaryAnn, but that is what she thought every time she stepped into the Laine's home next to the Fischers', or here into their motor home. Two summers ago, MaryAnn's dad had bought the big house on the hill as a summer home. Just recently he had given up politics and had moved his business to Richburg. Jodi was thrilled because it meant that MaryAnn would be in her tenth grade class at school this year.

MaryAnn ran water into two glasses, and Jodi glanced out the window toward Barkerville. There was no sign of the thin man.

"Oh, wow," she said with a sigh. "Now, where should I put this box?" She looked around the motor home and then accepted the water gratefully.

MaryAnn set her glass on the counter. "I know!" she said. "Over here, under the seat by the table." She went to the table and lifted the seat. Underneath was a small storage space that no one used. Jodi tucked the silver box inside.

"Hey! What are you guys doing?" Heather bounded into the motor home, and on her heels came Heidi. They were Jodi's six-year-old twin sisters.

Jodi realized they had seen her shutting the seat down. She turned to them.

"Oh, nothing," she replied casually and sat on the seat. "Have you had fun in Barkerville?"

Just then Mrs. Fischer came in.

"Everyone else went up to Richfield," she said. "Where have you girls been? Rustling up another mystery?" She grinned and got out the frying pan to fry hamburgers.

17

Jodi looked at MaryAnn and laughed nervously. "Well, I don't know if it's a mystery, but I did meet an old man. He's a real prospector, Mom, and he owns a cabin up beyond the town. I happened to find it when I was looking for Sugar."

Mrs. Fischer nodded. "That's nice. Now, would you girls mind peeling those carrots for dinner? And, Heather, you and Heidi can finish setting the table."

After supper everyone except Jodi, MaryAnn, and Brian decided to go see a film being shown at the museum. Jodi and MaryAnn cleaned up the kitchen and then sat at the picnic table outside. Brian was playing with Sugar.

Suddenly Jodi sat up. "Hey! There he is!" she exclaimed. "Over there! On the museum steps." She pointed toward an old man with a floppy, wide-brimmed hat on, slouching on the top step of the museum.

"There is *who?*" Brian asked. "Or aren't I supposed to know?" He pushed his blond hair off his forehead.

"Yeah. Who are you talking about, Jodi? All I see is an old man," MaryAnn said.

Jodi hit her forehead in exasperation. "Don't you remember? Joe! Joe the prospector, the owner of the silver box!"

MaryAnn straightened up. "Oh, Joe!" she said. "He looks sorta sad."

Brian sighed. "Joe *who*? And *what* silver box? I think something is going on!"

Jodi laughed. "I guess you can be in on it, Detective Fischer. Not really much of a mystery yet, though." As quickly as she could, she told Brian what had happened so far.

"And now I want to go over and talk to Joe," she said. She got up and began walking toward the museum, but MaryAnn tugged on her arm.

"Wait, Jodi," she said. "He looks so sad. Don't you think we ought to tell him about the Lord Jesus?"

18

Jodi paused, seeing the concern in MaryAnn's brown eyes.

"Well, I suppose, if we can—" her voice trailed off. MaryAnn had received the Lord as her Savior only last summer, and here she was the first to think of witnessing to Joe. Jodi felt like kicking herself.

Joe did not look up until they stopped right in front of him.

"Hi, Joe," Jodi said. Joe looked up and jumped. His shoulders straightened, and a grin spread across his face. He stood up and his blue eyes sparkled.

"Jodi!" he said. "I thought you had done gone by now." He turned to MaryAnn. "Is this here your friend?"

Jodi introduced MaryAnn and Brian, and then they walked to the picnic table beside the motor home. Jodi slipped into the motor home to put on her sweater because it was getting chilly outside, and MaryAnn came behind her to fix a snack for Joe.

"Here, this will help with the mosquitoes, too," Brian said as he set the mosquito repellent coil on the table and lit it. A thin cloud of blue smoke drifted lazily into the air.

"But, Joe," Jodi asked when they had served him some iced tea and cake. "How come you took the ladder down today and left me stranded in the attic?"

Joe's head dropped and he sighed. "I'm really sorry about that, but I figured a smart girl like you could find a way out of the attic. It was better than—" He paused.

"I—I cain't rightly tell you how it happened, Jodi. I guess you'll just have to trust me when I say it couldn't be helped. And someone came and stole that there letter I found of Pappy's."

Jodi gasped. "Stole it! But why would anyone else want it?"

"Well, the way I figure it," Joe drawled, "is that someone else knew about that box. Now, you see, that box

19

is mighty valuable, beings as it's made out of silver and has them jewels in it. And on top of that, it must be quite old by now. Yup—someone else must be after that box."

Brian pulled on Jodi's arm. "Hey! I betcha it was the guy you saw coming out of the woods just as you left the cabin!" he said.

"What'd you say, young fellar?" Joe asked, looking at him piercingly.

Jodi explained how she and MaryAnn had gone back to the cabin, found the box, and were followed through Barkerville. She started to stand up.

"Do you want it? I have it here in the motor home," she said.

Joe looked around nervously and waved his hand. "No, no, I—I, ah, cain't take it now. Someone might steal it. No, I think the best thing would be for you girls to keep it, for the time bein', anyway." He glanced into the fringe of the woods that bordered the picnic area. "I—I think I'd better be goin' now," he said.

MaryAnn looked at him intently and then placed her hand on his arm. Her words were soft.

"Joe, are you in trouble?"

He clasped his hands to keep them from shaking, and glanced at MaryAnn pleadingly. "Now, you girls don't go worryin' your heads about me. I ken take care of myself. And don't go to no police, neither. This business is just between you and me, OK?"

"We won't go to the police unless we have to, Joe," Jodi replied. "But sometimes we need others to help us, and especially we need the Lord. If you don't feel like you can talk to us about your problem, you can talk to the Lord."

Joe shook his head. "No, I cain't talk to the Lord. He wouldn't take two seconts for an old sinner like me." He sighed and put his forehead in his hands.

MaryAnn leaned forward. "You may be an old sinner, Joe, but God loves you just the same. I was a young sinner, and He saved me. God's Word says, 'For God so loved the world, that He gave His only begotten Son, that whosoever believes in Him should not perish, but have eternal life.' God loves you so much, Joe, that He sent His Son to die for the payment of your sin." She paused. Joe's head lifted, and he fastened his eyes on her eagerly.

"Seems how I remember a missionary tellin' me somethin' like that years ago. What does an old sinner like me do to get ahold of God's forgiveness?"

MaryAnn's eyes glistened as she continued. "That's the best part, Joe! God's forgiveness is free! We only need to ask for it, and believe God." She paused to dab her eyes.

Jodi spoke up. "The Bible says we need to confess our sin, and I guess that means that we agree with God that we have sinned, and then ask Him to forgive us in Jesus' name. And He will. And then He will be your friend, and you can talk to Him and ask Him to help you."

Joe nodded and his eyes were watery. "I see now," he said. "But I should be goin'. Are you stayin' here tonight?"

"No, we're going out to Bowron Lakes tonight, and we'll be at the Bowron Lakes Resort. Come out and see us, OK?" Jodi said sincerely. MaryAnn ran into the motor home and came out with a tract that explained the way of salvation.

Joe tucked the paper in his pocket, then stood up and walked across the parking lot toward Barkerville.

Jodi watched as he walked away. "Oh, I hope he *does* find the Lord as his Savior," she said softly.

Brian nodded. "So do I. But I'd like to see that box. Where is it?"

"In the motor home," Jodi said. "C'mon, we'll show it to you." She untied Sugar and carried her into the motor home with them. MaryAnn got the box from under the seat and laid it carefully on the table.

21

Brian picked it up, ran his finger over the design of the dragon, and looked inside.

"Somehow, it doesn't add up," Jodi said almost to herself, still looking at the box. "This box is valuable, but I think Joe's troubles are more than someone trying to steal it. I don't think he's telling everything."

MaryAnn nodded. "Oh, that's pretty clear. He never did tell us why he left you stranded in the attic. And have you noticed how he doesn't finish his sentences sometimes?"

"It all has to do with this box, though," Jodi said. She took the box from Brian and began looking at it closer. "I wonder if there isn't something else in here," she said.

"You mean like a hidden drawer, or something?" MaryAnn exclaimed excitedly, leaning closer to Jodi.

Suddenly Sugar began barking furiously at the door. Jodi jumped.

"Sugar!" she said. "Stop that barking! Hush!" The small dog paused in her barking and looked at Jodi. Then she began again. Jodi went over and picked her up, but still she barked and whined and pawed at Jodi.

Jodi went to the door, opened it, and looked out. Her heart was pounding. There was nothing. She listened for a few moments, then stepped back into the motor home, locking the door behind her. Was the man who followed them earlier spying on them from the woods? She shivered.

"Here it is!" Brian exclaimed. Jodi stepped over to the table and saw that Brian had found a secret compartment in the bottom of the box. By pushing a round spot, a little door opened to reveal a hidden drawer.

"Look! There's something in it!" Jodi said. She put Sugar down. "A piece of paper!" With shaking fingers she pulled a small piece of paper from the drawer. It was yellowed with age and very fragile. She spread it out on the table carefully.

MaryAnn pushed back her hair. "There's some writing on it," she said. "But I can't read it."

"That's because these are Chinese symbols," Jodi replied, leaning closely over the paper. "And some of them are underlined!"

Suddenly someone began banging frantically on the door. Jodi swept the box and the piece of paper off the table onto the seat beside her. Brian went to the door.

"Who is it?" he asked.

A small, frightened voice answered. "Heather! Let me in! Quick!" It sounded as if she were going to cry. Brian unlocked the door, and Heather bounded into the motor home.

Her brown braids were sticking out and her face was white. Her hand shook as she pointed toward the window facing the woods.

"There was a man standing right beside that window!"

3

A Shot Rings Out!

They all jumped to the window, pushed aside the frilly white curtains, and looked out. But no one was there. MaryAnn squatted down and put her arm around Heather to quiet her.

"Can you tell us all about it?" she asked softly, wiping the tears from the little girl's face.

Heather nodded. "I didn't like that movie," she said. "So Mom said I could come back here. I was coming across the parking lot and I thought I saw someone sneaking up by the motor home. But I wasn't sure, cuz I couldn't see the other side too good." She paused and sniffed.

"So I sorta snuck up and looked around the corner, and right in front of me there was a man. He was standing right by this window, like he was listening." They all looked at the window again.

"What did he look like?" Jodi asked. She gripped the table top tightly.

Heather shook her head. "I—I can't remember. Oh, I'm so scared, MaryAnn! Go get Daddy!" She threw her arms around MaryAnn and sobbed against her shoulder.

MaryAnn patted her. "It's OK now, Heather. Look at Sugar. She isn't barking anymore. That'sa girl. No more tears."

Heather smiled and scooped Sugar into her arms. Jodi stepped toward the door and opened it.

"Where are you going?" MaryAnn asked.

Jodi motioned toward the fringe of trees. "Just outside for a look. I'll be right back."

"I'm coming, too!" Brian said, and followed Jodi out the door.

24

She stepped outside and paused, studying the trees and bushes nearest the motor home. Was the sinister, dark-haired man peering at them? She glanced at Brian.

"Let's look for footprints or something he dropped that may give us a clue," she said. She began walking slowly around the motor home and then stepped into the fringe of trees. Brian was close behind her.

Suddenly she spotted a wadded up piece of paper lying on the ground. She leaned over and picked it up.

"Here's something," she said to Brian. She smoothed out the paper.

Brian leaned close. "What does it say?" he asked.

"Butt out," Jodi read. "That's all! That man who was listening must have written this while we were talking to Heather!" She tucked the note in her jeans pocket. "Let's look for something else."

Jodi shivered as she stepped deeper into the woods. The meaning of the message burned into her mind. Someone did not want them helping Joe! She clenched her fist. Well, it would not work! She was still going to try to help him. Just then Brian grunted.

"Here's something, sis," he said. "It was under that bush." He handed her a small black book. She opened it and flipped through the pages.

"An address book," she muttered. "Let's get back to the motor home. I have the spooky feeling that someone's watching us!" She glanced around and trotted back to the motor home.

Brian locked the door behind them, and Jodi settled down on the couch with a sigh of relief.

"Whew! I feel safer in here," she said. She brought out the note and the black book. MaryAnn read the scribbled note.

"Butt out," MaryAnn said. "What in the world—"

Jodi shook her head. "It must mean to leave Joe alone and mind our own business. I think that thin man wanted us to see that, but he must have dropped this by accident." She held up the black book and then began looking through it.

"It's an address and telephone book!" MaryAnn exclaimed.

Jodi nodded. "Look at the names and numbers. Most of them are in Langely. Oh! Here's one in Wells. That's the town just before we came to Barkerville."

"But who does it belong to?" MaryAnn asked.

Jodi turned to the first page. There, at the top, was a name scribbled so badly she could hardly make it out.

"Loui—no, that's a *J*. It's Joe—Joseph Carlen. Oh, that's a *T*. Carter. Joseph Carter."

"Is that Joe?" Brian asked.

Jodi shrugged her shoulders. "I don't know. But why would that man have Joe's address book?"

"Here comes Daddy and Mom!" Heather cried. She had been playing on the floor with Sugar. Jodi glanced out the window.

"I'll put these clues in the box," she said. "If you two will stand up."

Mr. Fischer, who was short and sandy-haired, held the door for Mrs. Fischer. Heidi came behind them.

Heather ran to her father. "Oh, Daddy! There was this man standing right by the motor home! There by the window! It scared me so much!"

Mr. Fischer looked at Jodi. "What's going on?" he asked.

"I really don't know, Dad," Jodi said innocently. "I didn't see him."

Mrs. Fischer gazed at Jodi. "Is that all, Jodi?" she asked. "Sure there isn't another mystery going on?"

Jodi squirmed. "Well, yes, there is, sort of. It has to do with that old man we met today. I think he's in some kind of trouble, and I'd like to try to help him." She looked at her father appealingly.

He smiled a bit. "You must have a special gift for smelling out mysterious situations, Jodi. But I want you to exercise some caution this time. You have my permission to help this old man, but I want you to be careful and let us know where you are and what you are doing. Is that clear?"

"But, Dad, I—" Jodi began, but just then Mr. Laine came into the motor home and announced they should be going to Bowron Lakes. Mrs. Fischer, Jodi, and Mary-Ann became very busy closing cupboards and putting things away for the trip.

Soon they were driving down the winding dirt road that led to Bowron Lakes.

Mrs. Fischer sat at the table across from MaryAnn and sighed. "I sure wish your mom could have come, MaryAnn. It would have been good for her to get away."

"I know." MaryAnn nodded. "But she just couldn't see taking Mark into this wilderness." Jodi smiled as she thought of the Laine's newly adopted baby son.

"Bowron Lakes Resort." Jodi read the sign a little later as they drove off the main road and down to a small building that was the resort office. She could see small cabins scattered along the lake.

They stopped and everyone got out.

"Oh, look at those mountains!" Mrs. Fischer exclaimed. Across the blue waters of the lake were jagged, snow-capped mountains.

Jodi drew a deep breath of the piney mountain air. It was good to be here, but she wondered sadly if she had not left the mystery of the silver box behind in Barkerville.

Just then Mr. Laine came out of the office.

"The cabin we're renting is just down that road a little way," he said, pointing to a small road that wound through the trees.

Mrs. Fischer nodded. "Oh, that's fine. The girls and I will walk. We need the exercise." She grinned and took Jodi's arm.

Jodi groaned. "I don't need the exercise," she said. "I've been walking all over Barkerville!" But the men had piled into the motor home and had started the engine. Jodi followed reluctantly behind her mother. Her legs were tired, and her head ached.

Suddenly she heard a loud noise and turned to look back toward the store. An old, rattle-trap truck had just pulled up to the office in a cloud of dust. A short, bearded man with a huge stomach got out and walked into the store. There was another man in the truck, but she could not see his face.

"Jodi, it's impolite to stare," Mrs. Fischer called to her from down the road. "Come on!"

Their cabin was a tiny log structure tucked among the trees, only a stone's throw from the lake. Jodi explored the two bedrooms and the tiny living-room-kitchen and then helped unpack their belongings. Afterward, she and MaryAnn sat on the front porch. The lake was perfectly still and all was quiet except the buzzing of mosquitoes. After exploring the woods and the cabin, Sugar settled herself at Jodi's feet.

Jodi sprayed some stinky repellent on herself and made a face.

"Well, it's not my choice of perfume," she said dryly, "but we're less likely to be eaten alive by those pests."

MaryAnn nodded, her eyes on the quiet lake. "It's so beautiful here. I'm glad we came." She paused. "I know! Let's sing. I'll get my guitar." She got her guitar from the motor home and settled on the top step with it on her knees.

Jodi enjoyed singing with MaryAnn, and before long, the rest of the family had gathered around and were singing, too. Mr. Laine gazed out to the lake. The long northern twilight was beginning to fade, and it was far too late for the twins to be up, but no one wanted to break the magic of the moment.

They had just begun another song when Jodi looked up, surprised. A tall, graying man had stepped around the corner of the cabin. Everyone stopped singing and Mr. Laine stood up. He introduced the man as Mr. Thompson, the owner of the resort. Sugar began to bark, but Jodi laid her hand on her head.

Mr. Thompson smiled and glanced at Jodi and Mary-Ann. "That was really fine singing," he said. "Couldn't help but hear it. Sound really carries on still evenings like this."

MaryAnn nodded. "We really like to sing."

"Well, it sure sounds good, and I was wondering if you two girls would do me a little favor," he said. "I like to have a little campfire down by the lake for my guests, and I think it would be great to take all this nice singing down there. Would you girls mind doing that?"

"I guess so," MaryAnn said slowly. She glanced at Jodi. "That is, if Jodi wants to."

Jodi cleared her throat. Everyone was looking at her. The fact was that she did *not* want to!

"Well, I—ah—I really don't feel too good," she said. "I have this headache." She paused and looked at her mother. "Maybe tomorrow night."

Brian turned to Jodi. "You can do it," he said. "You just don't want to."

An angry retort was on the tip of her tongue, but she held it back. Mr. Fischer stood up.

"I'm sure we can come up with something," he said to Mr. Thompson. "We'll be down there in fifteen minutes."

Mr. Thompson thanked him and left. Jodi took Sugar up in her lap.

"I really don't feel like it, Mom," she said. "My throat sort of hurts and I can't carry a tune when I'm in front of people. Why don't you sing with MaryAnn? You've got a lot better voice than I do."

"Chicken!" Brian taunted.

"Why, you little—" Jodi turned to him, her blue eyes flashing angrily.

"All right, you two!" Mr. Fischer interrupted. He looked at Jodi. "Jodi, we're not going to force you to sing with MaryAnn, but I want you to think about the

29

opportunity this will be for you to witness for the Lord."

MaryAnn put her guitar down. "If you're not singing, I'm not either," she said.

Jodi sighed, and rubbed her head. "Well, all right. But if I goof it up, it's not my fault!"

A fire was burning by the shore when they arrived a few minutes later. Some people were already there, and Jodi could see two more coming from the other side of the resort. There were chunks of wood and planks between them for seats.

Mr. Thompson came with an armload of firewood. He dumped it down and then brushed off his clothes. Jodi avoided looking at the other guests and bit her fingernails nervously. The smoke swirled around and got in her eyes, so she shifted positions. MaryAnn sat calmly on the other side of the fire, chatting with an older lady. She thought bitterly that she could be calm, too, if she had a good singing voice like MaryAnn's.

Mr. Thompson was standing up now. "I want this to be a real friendly time," he announced. "So let's go around and introduce ourselves, and then I have a special treat for you."

Beside Jodi's and MaryAnn's families, there was an older, grayhaired lady named Mrs. Christy, and a Chinese family named the Fongs who had a girl Jodi's age. Sitting toward the back and farther out of the campfire light were two men.

Mr. Thompson asked for their names.

"Uh—Alan Young," the one with the big stomach replied. "And this here's m' buddy, Shorty." He nudged the other man who had a big cowboy hat pulled down on his forehead. Everyone laughed.

"Great!" Mr. Thompson said. He replenished the fire and a shower of sparks flew up. He glanced at Mary-Ann.

"And now to introduce our special guests tonight, Jodi and MaryAnn. They do some fine singing and guitar playing. It's a little different than what most kids sing,

30

but I think you'll like it." He paused. "You're on, girls."

Jodi was afraid and unsure of herself, so the first song was wobbly and a little off key. But by the time she and MaryAnn sang two more songs and then taught a simple chorus to the people, she was more comfortable and her voice blended smoothly with MaryAnn's alto. They were singing their last number when the man with the big cowboy hat looked directly at Jodi.

Suddenly Jodi knew where she'd seen him before. The words of the song stuck in her throat. MaryAnn continued singing alto, and finally Jodi joined her again.

After the singing and some friendly chatter, Mrs. Christy invited the Fischers and the Laines to her cabin for coffee.

Mrs. Fischer smiled, but shook her head. "I have to put some sleepy girls to bed," she said. "I'd love to come tomorrow, though."

Mrs. Christy, who was small and slender with sparkly brown eyes and quick movements, patted Mrs. Fischer's arm. "Oh, that's fine. How about the rest of you?"

Mr. Fischer shook his head. "I think we'd better hit the sack, too. We're heading out first thing in the morning to canoe around the lakes."

"Then that leaves you two," Mrs. Christy said to MaryAnn and Jodi. "And I'll change the menu to hot chocolate and doughnuts. How about it?"

Jodi smiled. She liked Mrs. Christy right away. "Sure! But my weary bones tell me we won't be able to stay long."

It had become quite dark, so Mrs. Christy turned on her little pocket flashlight, and the three followed a trail through the woods to her cabin. She let the girls in and began heating the milk.

Jodi glanced at the open Bible on the table. "Are you a Christian?" she asked.

"Yes, I sure am, and I take it you girls are, too," Mrs. Christy answered. She smiled and her eyes lit up. "How about your parents?"

31

Jodi nodded. "My parents are—they are missionaries to the Indian people. But MaryAnn's aren't, yet. We're praying they will receive Christ soon."

Mrs. Christy smiled and added the chocolate to the milk. "I'm sure they will—I just love it up here. I come up every summer to think and write. My husband died five years ago from cancer." She poured the hot drink and then sat down with the girls. "Now you tell me about yourselves," she said.

An hour later, Jodi and MaryAnn were using the flashlight Mrs. Christy had loaned them to find their way back to their cabin. The woods were dark and the trees towered over them like giant guards of the forest.

"It's scary," Jodi said, glancing into the shadows. She could imagine a dark-haired man sneaking up behind them. "Let's hurry!"

MaryAnn grabbed Jodi's arm. "Hey, slow down! I want to stay near that light. And how come you quit singing on the last song?"

Jodi groaned. "Oh, that was awful! I knew I would mess things up. I was off key all night!"

"Why did you stop singing?" MaryAnn repeated.

Jodi stopped. "Because I suddenly realized who that man was, that was sitting in the back and had a big cowboy hat on. He looked right at me, and I'm sure he was the one who followed us in Barkerville!"

MaryAnn gripped Jodi's arm. Her voice shook. "How—how could you be so sure?" she whispered.

"I got a good look at him in Barkerville," Jodi whispered. "I *know* it's the same man, and he's followed us here! Let me tell you, MaryAnn, whatever Joe's trouble is, I'm afraid we've inherited it!" She shivered.

MaryAnn took the flashlight. "Well, let's get home!"

The next morning before the sun was up, Jodi heard whispering and heavy footsteps in the next room. She and MaryAnn had slept in one of the bedrooms of the cabin. She put on a robe and stumbled out into the other room.

32

Mr. Fischer was just closing the door. When he saw her, he opened it again.

"Up already, sweetheart?" he asked. "We're just leaving. Now you be good and go easy on your mom. Not too many mysteries until we get back."

Jodi grinned. "Bye, Dad. I'll come and see you off." She slipped on her shoes and followed him to the dock where the canoe was loaded with their supplies. It would take five days to canoe around the chain of lakes. Brian sat bright-eyed and excited in the middle of the canoe.

"Hey, Jodi!" he called. "Don't solve that mystery till I get back, OK?"

They pushed away from the dock.

"Time and mysteries wait for no man," Jodi called back across the water. "Or little boys!"

Later that morning after the dishes were done and the cabin and motor home straightened, Jodi and Mary-Ann walked over to the office. Sugar tagged along at Jodi's feet.

Mr. Thompson looked up as they came in and a smile flitted across his face.

"We'd like to get to know that Chinese girl," Jodi said, picking up Sugar. "Could you tell us where their cabin is?"

His smile widened. "Sure. You girls did a great job last night. Want to try a skit or something for tonight?" He led the way outside and pointed out the Fong's cabin.

MaryAnn nodded. "I think we can come up with something," she said. "And thanks for the directions."

Jodi tousled Sugar's white, fluffy coat and then put her down.

"Maybe Mr. Fong can tell us what is written on that note we found in the silver box," she said. "I put it in my pocket."

Susan Fong answered the door when Jodi knocked.

Jodi smiled. "Hi."

The Chinese girl looked down shyly. "Hi," she said.

Jodi felt uncomfortable and wondered how to get a conversation going.

Just then Sugar bounded up the steps, barking at Susan. Jodi picked her up.

"Hush, Sugar!" She glanced at Susan. "I'm so sorry. She doesn't have very good manners."

A smile spread over Susan's face. "Oh, what a cute puppy!" She patted the little dog. "And you call her Sugar?"

Jodi nodded and grinned. "Because she's white."

MaryAnn moved forward. "You have a nice view of the lake from here," she said. "I think your cabin is higher than ours."

Susan lifted her head and nodded. "It is nice here." She paused. "Here, have a chair. I'll get some tea. My mom and dad went shopping in Wells, but they should be back soon."

She disappeared into the cabin and came back shortly with glasses of iced tea.

A little later, when there was a pause in the conversation, Jodi drew the yellowed paper from her pocket and spread it out on her lap. She pulled her chair closer to Susan's.

"Look what we found yesterday in an old Chinese box," she said. "I think this must be Chinese writing. Can you read it?"

Susan studied the paper. "It looks very old. But I haven't learned to read Chinese yet, much to the despair of my father."

Just then Sugar began barking near some bushes down by the lake. Jodi stood up and called to her.

"Dumb dog." She sighed and sat back down. "Probably just a—"

Then they all heard a strange whining noise, a soft thud behind them, then the loud explosion of a gun!

4

"My Birthday Is Saturday!"

"That was a shot!" Jodi exclaimed. She grabbed Sugar's collar as the dog came panting up onto the porch.

MaryAnn jumped up. "Look! It must have hit the cabin!" She pointed to a fresh mark in the old wood just above their heads.

"If we had been standing up, that could have hit us!" Jodi replied, glancing out to the lake. Suddenly she heard a sighing sound behind her. She whirled and saw Susan standing up, her face pale and her hand on her stomach.

"I—I don't feel so good," she said. She crumpled to the floor.

"She's fainted!" Jodi said and stared at her.

MaryAnn knelt beside the girl, straightened out her feet, and laid her head on a cushion.

"Hurry and get some water, Jodi," MaryAnn said. "And get a blanket or something I can put over her."

Jodi rushed blindly into the cabin and ripped a quilt off of the bed. She looked around for water, but the bucket was empty. She grabbed it and ran out to Mary-Ann.

MaryAnn had Susan's feet raised and adjusted the blanket over her. Jodi ran down the path to the lake. Then she heard a noise on the lake just around a point of land. It sounded as if someone were starting a motor boat!

A few seconds later, a boat came from around the bend in the lake. There was a man in it, but he was hunched over the motor. The boat was green, and there were words on it, but she could not make them out. It looked as if the man wore a floppy, wide-brimmed hat.

"Jodi!" MaryAnn called from the cabin. "Hurry up!" She jumped and turned to fill the bucket in the lake.

When Jodi came back to the cabin, MaryAnn dipped a facecloth in the water and laid it gently on Susan's forehead.

Susan's eyes fluttered and then opened. She tried to sit up but MaryAnn gently forced her back.

"That's OK, Susan," she said. "Just lie down and rest a bit." She glanced up at Jodi. "I'll stay with her—why don't you go to the office and tell Mr. Thompson what happened? Maybe he'll know how to get hold of her parents."

Susan began sobbing. Jodi jumped off the porch and ran down the path to the office. Sugar, thinking Jodi was playing, frisked around her feet and almost tripped her. Jodi burst into the little building, her breath coming in gasps.

"Mr. Thompson! Susan! There was a shot—she fainted—gotta get hold of her parents!" She paused for breath, and Mr. Thompson came closer and put his hand on her shoulder.

"Slow down a bit," he said calmly. "Tell me what happened."

Jodi took a deep breath and related all that had just happened. His face grew stern as she talked. When she finished, he took two big steps to the telephone and began dialing.

"Nothing like that's ever happened here before," he muttered angrily. "Can't understand it. Crazy hunters. Oh, hello!" He continued talking and then replaced the phone. "That was the police detachment at Wells. They're sending out an officer right away, and they'll also be on the lookout for the Fong's car. Now, I'll go with you to their cabin as soon as I call my daughter to look after things here."

When they got back to the cabin, Susan was lying on her bed, conscious, but her face was still very pale. She seemed relieved to see Mr. Thompson.

"Well, it looks like MaryAnn knows what she's doing," Mr. Thompson commented as he walked across the cabin and stood by Susan's bed. "How are you feeling, Susan?"

She nodded and tried to smile. "I'm OK," she said. "I have never fainted before. It's—it's just that I got so scared—" She began sobbing again with her hands on her face.

MaryAnn jumped up and patted her arm. "That's OK, Susan," she soothed. "Just try not to think of it. I'm sure your parents will be here any moment."

"Yes, and the police, too," Mr. Thompson agreed. He sat down on a chair and changed the subject. Jodi kept glancing out the window. What was taking them so long? After a while, she stood and paced to the door. Then she heard voices. She motioned to Mr. Thompson and they stepped out onto the porch.

The Fongs were hurrying toward the cabin, and behind them were two Royal Canadian Mounted Police officers. One of them was carrying a small black briefcase. Mr. Thompson explained briefly to Susan's parents what had happened as they hurried into the cabin.

MaryAnn stepped out onto the porch and pushed her long, dark hair back from her face. Jodi thought longingly that it must be nice to always know the right thing to do.

A tall, blond officer turned to Jodi and MaryAnn. "I'm Officer Davis, and this is Officer Roth. Now, I want the full story, with all the details," he said.

Jodi told the story and Officer Roth jotted down notes in a small notebook. The policemen dug the bullet out of the wall, then walked down the path to the bushes where Sugar had been barking just before the shot.

The two policemen searched the area carefully and finally Officer Davis stood up.

"Here it is, Joe," he exclaimed and held up the cartridge from the bullet. "Rifle. Looks like a thirty-aught-six. Got an envelope?" Officer Roth pulled an envelope out of the briefcase, put the bullet and cartridge inside, and marked the outside.

Jodi told them about seeing a man in a motor boat coming from behind the point of land. The officers had her describe him and the boat as best as she could. They walked down the beach, the officers staring intently at the ground. Suddenly they stopped.

"Here!" Officer Roth said. "Here are some clear ones."

Sugar bounded from the bushes along the beach and frisked around Jodi's feet. Then she started toward the policemen.

"Keep that dog back!" Officer Davis barked, shielding something on the ground from Sugar's prancing feet. Jodi grabbed her collar and watched the officers.

"We've found some clear footprints, and they may belong to the man who shot at you," Officer Davis explained more calmly. "We can't risk getting them messed up."

Officer Roth took out a small camera from the briefcase, adjusted the distance, and took several pictures of the footprint. Officer Davis thanked Jodi and said he would let Mr. Thompson know if they found the man.

Later, as Jodi and MaryAnn hurried to their own cabin, Jodi sighed.

"Wow, what a deal," she said. "We'd better hurry. It's past lunchtime and I bet Mom is wondering why we were gone so long!" She whistled for Sugar.

MaryAnn nodded. "I suppose so. I feel so sorry for Susan. I've never seen anyone so upset!"

"It's my fault," Jodi said. "And I just stood and stared when she fainted. I wish I wasn't so stupid!" She stooped down to pick up her bouncy white puppy.

MaryAnn gave her a little push. "Oh, Jodi, stop it! You know it wasn't your fault! You just think about yourself too much."

They started down the narrow drive to the cabin. Jodi ran her fingers through her red brown hair and sighed again. MaryAnn's words cut deep into her heart. *It's true,* she thought. *I am selfish, unkind—*

38

She stopped suddenly as the bushes crackled beside her and a man stepped out onto the path. Sugar leaped from her arms and began barking furiously.

"Oh!" Jodi squealed and jumped back. Then she realized it was Joe standing in front of them, his weather-beaten face half hidden under the floppy, wide-brimmed hat he always wore.

He smiled. "Sorry to scare you girls like that," he drawled. "Been awaitin' here for ya to come."

"Oh, hi, Joe," Jodi answered when she got her breath. She hushed Sugar.

Joe glanced over his shoulder. "I gotta be goin'. Someone's been watchin' and trailin' me. But I wanted to see you again."

Jodi leaned forward. "Do you want the box, Joe?" she whispered.

"No, no. You girls keep it for me now," he said. He clenched his hands together. "Keep it real good, OK? Someone might want to steal it!"

Jodi touched his arm, concern in her blue eyes. "Isn't there anything else we can do for you? We found this paper in the box, and it has some—"

"Sh!" Joe hissed. "Don't talk about it now. I gotta go." He glanced in the woods. "I'll need it soon. But, listen. You girls did help me." He straightened up and smiled. "I read that paper and I did what it said. I guess I got God's forgiveness now, cuz my heart shore does feel clean!"

Jodi's heart gave a leap of joy. Impulsively she hugged the old man. MaryAnn shook his hand.

"Oh, Joe!" Jodi said. "That's so neat! Do you have a Bible? Come on down to the cabin and I'll give you one."

Joe smiled but shook his head. "No, I better go now. I—I was hopin' so much I could help you all with your Indian work," he said. "Always wanted to do somethin' fine and noble." He sighed and shook his head. "But it doesn't look like I'll be able to. My birthday's

Saturday, ya see, and—" He paused, listening.

"But, Joe, what does that have to do with anything?" Jodi asked.

Joe shook his head. "I can't tell you now," he whispered. "I gotta go. Watch the box—be careful—there's a clue in there to my father's—" He paused. A twig snapped close by in the woods. The old man glanced around and then dashed away.

Jodi and MaryAnn stared at each other.

"What in the world—" MaryAnn said.

Jodi turned and trotted down the road. "Let's get out of here!" she said.

Mrs. Fischer wanted a full report of their activities and was concerned about Susan and the shooting at the cabin. Jodi and MaryAnn ate a quick lunch and then went to the motor home to talk. Heather and Heidi had lain down for naps, and Mrs. Fischer said she wanted to read.

"You know, Jodi," MaryAnn said, munching on an apple, "we ought to write everything down that's happened so far. I'm so confused, and maybe we've missed something important that would help us understand what's going on."

Jodi bit into her own apple and nodded. "That's a good idea," she said. "And since you thought of it, you can do it."

MaryAnn found some paper and a pen; then she and Jodi tried to remember everything about the mystery.

"Now, what did Joe say to you the very first time you met him?" MaryAnn asked, her pen poised.

"Well, that he comes up here and pans gold in the summer, and that he always wanted to do something really good." Jodi paused. "And then he said, 'Maybe there's a way, if only I could find—,' but he never finished."

MaryAnn looked up. "That's a clue," she commented. "Joe wants to find something."

"But I just assumed he wanted to find the silver box," Jodi replied, a puzzled look in her blue eyes.

40

MaryAnn shook her head. "But when you found the box, he didn't want it. I think he meant he wants to find something else."

Jodi nodded. "Something bigger, maybe. But what?"

"I don't know." MaryAnn shrugged. "But let's go on writing things down."

They talked about finding the box and the man who followed them in Barkerville.

MaryAnn paused in her writing and glanced up. "You mean, *if* he was following us. I think it was your imagination, Jodi."

Jodi groaned. "Oh, MaryAnn. You wouldn't believe me if he came up and clobbered us! But we do know someone else is wise to Joe's plans, because someone stole his father's letter and someone wrote us a warning note at Barkerville."

"Hold on!" MaryAnn waved her hand. "I can't write that fast!" She scribbled furiously for a few minutes. "Now, what else? I have up to the time when we came here."

Jodi put her apple core in the wastebasket under the sink.

"Well, there are two suspects here at the resort, and shortly after they came, someone shot at us!"

MaryAnn sighed and rolled her eyes toward the ceiling. "Jodi! You don't know for sure if those guys are connected with this. And we have no way of knowing who shot at us."

"I said *suspects*," Jodi shot back. "I know that little one is the guy who followed us in Barkerville. Just write it down."

She drummed her fingers on the table. *Why must MaryAnn be such a know-it-all? Everything has to go her way!*

MaryAnn glanced at Jodi. "You're getting mad, aren't you? Well, I didn't mean to be so smart-aleck. Now, describe that boat you saw."

"It was green, MaryAnn. You know that. And the

41

man had on a floppy hat—like the one Joe wears."

MaryAnn's brown eyes widened. "Like Joe's! Jodi! That might have been Joe!"

"No, it couldn't. The boat took off down the lake. A little later we saw Joe in the bushes here at the resort. He couldn't have had time to get back here." She paused. "I don't think so, anyway. But why would he want to shoot at us?"

MaryAnn waved her pen at Jodi. "Maybe Joe is wanted by the police. Maybe that's why he's so jumpy. Maybe we're trying to help a criminal!"

"Now who's jumping to conclusions?" Jodi laughed. She stood up. "No, I think Joe is on the level. He wasn't trying to hide anything the first time I met him— you know, I have the feeling we should hide the box and the note better."

MaryAnn stood up and took the box from under the seat. "I've been nervous about them being in here, too. But where?"

"Let's take care of this paper first," Jodi said and took out the yellowed paper from her pocket. "And I know where to hide it." She opened a drawer where her Bible was kept and laid it on the table. Next she found some tape and then turned to the maps in the back of the Bible.

"I'm going to tape this into my Bible, back here in the maps," she said, and grinned. "Who would look for it back here?"

MaryAnn studied the paper as Jodi taped it down. Suddenly she sat up.

"Hey! Look at this! I never saw this before." She pointed at some faint scribblings at the very bottom of the paper.

Jodi leaned over. "What does it say? It's so faded. Hm—I think that first word is 'mother.' "

"And this here is the capital letter *L*," MaryAnn put in.

42

Jodi frowned. "*Mother L.* What do you suppose it means?"

"I don't know, Jodi." MaryAnn sighed. "Now, where shall we hide the silver box? It's a little harder, you know."

Jodi sat down to think. "Let's see, a place where no one would ever look for it." She rubbed her forehead and then ran her fingers through her curly hair. Suddenly she jumped up.

"Oh, I know! Get a hammer, MaryAnn, and follow me!"

MaryAnn hurriedly pulled out several drawers and finally picked up a hammer. Jodi led the way outside, through the bushes down a little path, and came to a small building. MaryAnn looked at Jodi in surprise.

"The outhouse?"

Jodi grinned. "A place where no one would *ever* look for it!" She and MaryAnn crowded inside and closed the door.

MaryAnn held her nose. "Just hurry up," she said. "The aroba id here isd't the greatest."

"You're a city slicker!" Jodi laughed. "But, look. There's a loose board here. I think the box will fit between the outside wall and the inside wall, if I can squeeze it in."

She pulled the loose board a little further away from the stud and carefully lowered the silver box into the space between the two walls. MaryAnn flapped her hands at the flies while Jodi hammered the board back in again.

When she and MaryAnn returned to the motor home, Mrs. Fischer and the twins were just starting down the hill for the lake. Sugar was running at their heels. Mrs. Fischer stopped.

"Oh, Jodi! There you are!" she called. Jodi ran down the hill. Her mother continued. "I was just taking Heidi and Heather for a ride in a boat, but now that you are here, you can do it. OK?"

43

"Sure, Mom," Jodi replied. "What boat should I take?"

Mrs. Fischer waved toward the resort dock. "Oh, I'm sure they rent boats from the resort. Here's some money. Just don't be gone too long, and take it easy, OK?" She started back up to the cabin and called Sugar.

Jodi picked out a small rowboat with a motor on it. Mr. Thompson leaned over and pulled the starter rope. The motor sputtered to life. He showed Jodi how to adjust the throttle, then shut it off.

"Now, you start it," he said.

Jodi looked at him uncertainly. She leaned over and yanked hard on the rope. Nothing happened. She tried again. Still nothing. Mr. Thompson smiled.

"Put more snap into it," he said. "You can't take it out unless you can start it."

Jodi's arm ached, but finally she got the hang of it, and the motor coughed, sputtered, and then roared to life. They waved and headed out over the choppy lake.

Jodi turned the boat in the direction that she had seen the man who had shot at them go. Heidi and Heather laughed and dipped their hands into the water that was splashing up over the sides. The lake was not so rough closer to shore, so Jodi steered toward land. They rounded several points and explored the inlets. On the far side of one point was another resort. The sign at the end of the dock said Green Haven Resort. There were several rowboats tied to the dock.

Jodi swung in closer. Just what she expected! The boats were green!

"Look at the boats!" she called to MaryAnn over the roar of the motor. But MaryAnn only glanced at them, nodded, and smiled.

"Better head back," she said. "Don't want to run out of gas!"

Jodi shook her head. "Mr. Thompson filled it when we left!"

Heidi caught herself in the middle of a sentence and

44

looked at Jodi. "What if we run out of gas?" she asked soberly.

"I guess we'd have to row," Jodi said. "Don't worry." But she turned the boat back.

About halfway back, the motor coughed, sputtered, and then died. Jodi swung around on the seat and pulled the cord. Nothing happened. She tried again. Still nothing.

Heidi's mouth pulled down at the corners and she began sniffing. "We're stuck!" she sobbed. "I want to go home!"

Heather fought the tears and patted her sister's arm. "Don't cry, silly," she said. "Jodi will get it going. Won't you, Jodi?"

But Jodi did not answer. Her arm ached as she tried again and again to start the motor. Finally MaryAnn carefully crawled to the back of the boat and tried to start the motor. But still it remained silent.

Jodi sighed. "Well, I guess we better dig out the oars." The twins began crying. Jodi patted Heidi. "Don't cry. It will take a little longer, but we'll get there. If you are real quiet, maybe we'll see a beaver or something!" The twins dried their eyes and began searching the shoreline.

"I guess I'll be first," MaryAnn said. She crawled to the center seat and fitted the oars in the oarlocks. She began with strong strokes, but it was not long before she tired out and traded places with Jodi.

"We shouldn't be too far," she said hopefully. "Maybe around the next point of land."

Jodi sat facing the shore, looking beyond MaryAnn's head into the woods. She saw an old deserted cabin on the shore not far away. She stared at it. There! What was that? A movement in the dark shadows of the cabin? Goosebumps covered her arms.

Then she saw a face, clearly outlined against the dark window. It was a man, a man with a mean scowl on his face!

5

The Legend of the Green-Eyed Dragon

"Oh!" Jodi screamed. "MaryAnn! There was the face of a man in that cabin up there!"

MaryAnn whirled around and stared at the cabin. But the face was gone. All was quiet for a few seconds. Then MaryAnn turned back.

"Get to rowing, Jodi," she whispered. "I don't like the looks of this place."

Heidi began crying again, and Heather was whimpering. Both girls huddled together in the end of the boat, their brown heads close.

"I want Mommy," Heidi sobbed.

Jodi said nothing, using all her strength to pull on the oars. Slowly they moved around the inlet and the point of land. MaryAnn sighed.

"We're OK, now," she said. "Heidi! Don't cry, sweetheart. We'll be back soon. See how fast Jodi is making the boat go?"

Heidi dried her tears but still clung to Heather. Jodi clenched her teeth against the terrible pain in her arms. Her hands were raw.

MaryAnn glanced at her reproachfully. "Really, Jodi," she said softly. "That was a silly thing to do, frightening the twins so much. I think it was just your imagination, anyway."

Jodi did not take time to answer, but MaryAnn's words seared her heart like a hot iron. It was true! She should not have said anything until later. She bit her lip and took another stroke, trying to ignore the pain in her arms and hands. Tears squeezed out of her eyes. Why couldn't she do anything right?

Another stroke, pain, tears. Another stroke.

They rounded a point of land, and the twins cheered as they saw the resort nestled in the cove. Jodi paused for a second and MaryAnn leaned forward.

"Want me to take it?" she asked.

Jodi shook her head. "I'm all right," she replied stubbornly. "Almost there now."

Mrs. Fischer was standing on the dock when they rowed up. Jodi sat in the boat, slowly uncurling her stiff fingers from the oars and taking deep gulps of air. Mary-Ann and the twins got out and tied the boat. Mr. Thompson came down the path from the office.

"Ran out of gas!" he exclaimed. "The tank was full when you left. You weren't gone long enough to run it dry. Let me see that motor."

Jodi scrambled out of the boat.

"Ha! Look at this!" he said, holding up a hose. "The gas line. It looks like it's been punctured. On purpose." He shook his head. "More work of pranksters. This just doesn't seem to be my week."

"It's me!" Jodi said bitterly. "I'm your bad luck."

Mr. Thompson smiled and brushed back his graying hair. "No, I'm sure it's not you, Jodi. But I am going to report this to the police."

Mrs. Fischer, the twins, and MaryAnn went up the path to the office, but Jodi turned to walk slowly down the beach. She rubbed her hands gently and sighed. What a mess things were in! She wished suddenly she could quietly disappear from the landscape. Tears filled her eyes and she stumbled over a rock on the shore. She looked up and then stopped.

Sitting on a log not far away was Mrs. Christy, her graying hair pulled smoothly back, her brown eyes smiling.

"Hello, Jodi," she said quietly. "Isn't it lovely out here?"

Jodi brushed the tears from her eyes and sat down beside Mrs. Christy. Together they were silent, soaking

47

in the deep beauty of the trees, the lake, the mountains. Tiny waves lapped gently on the beach, and Jodi could hear a squirrel scolding in the forest.

Finally Mrs. Christy turned to her and laid her hand on Jodi's arm.

"Now tell me, my dear, what's troubling you?" Her voice was gentle, and her manner loving and kind.

Jodi gazed out over the water, her blue eyes troubled. "I—I don't really know how to tell you," she said slowly. She glanced at Mrs. Christy and saw she was quietly listening. She gained confidence to continue.

"I guess it's *me,* really. I always get things into such a mess. And I can't do anything right. When Susan fainted this morning, MaryAnn knew exactly what to do, but all I could do was stand there and stare at her!" She paused and Mrs. Christy waited for her to go on. Her words flowed out freely now.

"I'm always trying to help people, you know, but the more I try to help, the worse things get. And I'm always blabbing my mouth and saying the wrong things. Like just now, I saw a face in the window of a cabin, and I had to scare the twins by saying something about it—I don't know, sometimes I feel so worthless, like I should just do everyone a favor by quietly disappearing somewhere. I don't think anyone would miss me." She cupped her chin in her hand.

Mrs. Christy smiled and stroked her well-worn Bible.

"I know just how you feel, Jodi," she said. "You see, I used to feel that very same way. In fact, I carried that feeling with me all of my life, until just five years ago—" She paused, her eyes following the movements of a loon out on the lake.

Jodi sat up. "What happened five years ago?"

"Two very beautiful things, Jodi," Mrs. Christy answered. "My husband went home to be with the Lord—" She smiled when she saw Jodi's eyes widen in surprise.

"Yes, Jodi, my husband's home-going was beautiful. God used it in so many ways. And in my own life, too.

I know he's so much better off now. The other thing that happened was being able to go to a seminar for women, where I learned to accept myself as God made me."

She opened her Bible and flipped the pages. "Did you know that God designed you just as you are? He made that pert little nose and those beautiful blue eyes. He made your hair curly and your personality like it is. Do you question the Master Artist on His design?"

Jodi looked down. "I—I never thought of it like that, I guess," she said.

"Look at these verses, Jodi," Mrs. Christy continued. "In fact, it would be good for you to memorize all of Psalm 139. Just read it for me, now. I love to hear it."

Jodi read clearly and quietly, not really taking notice of the words. Then she began to hear what she was reading.

"I will praise thee," she read. "For I am fearfully and wonderfully made: marvelous are thy works; and that my soul knoweth right well. My substance was not hid from thee, when I was made in secret, and curiously wrought in the lowest parts of the earth. Thine eyes did see my substance, yet being unperfect; and in thy book all my members were written, which in continuance were fashioned, when as yet there was none of them." She paused.

"How precious also are thy thoughts unto me, O God! how great is the sum of them!" She stopped reading and glanced up.

"Isn't that beautiful?" Mrs. Christy smiled, her face shining. "At that seminar we were taught that we should thank God for the way He made us, even the things we don't like about ourselves. And we should ask Him to forgive us for being bitter for making us the way He did. And then, we need to accept ourselves and agree with God that we will work *with* Him, not against Him. Because He isn't finished with you yet, Jodi, or with me either."

Jodi nodded. "I guess not. But I feel so dumb sometimes!"

"I know," Mrs. Christy replied. "But why do you feel dumb? Is it because you are comparing yourself with someone else? Did you know the Bible says that that is a very unwise thing to do? No, God made you special, Jodi. When those feelings come, thank God again for making you the way you are."

Jodi thought about that for a moment, nodded her head, and smiled. "I guess you're right," she said and stood up. I'll read this chapter again and pray about it. Thanks so much for talking with me! I feel so much better now!" She said good-bye and walked on down the beach.

That evening the campfire crackled merrily as Jodi and MaryAnn stood behind some bushes getting ready to do their skit. Mrs. Fischer held Jodi's purse in which she had put her Bible. MaryAnn had found a banana somewhere and had borrowed a coat.

Jodi peeked around the bush and saw another family arrive. Suddenly her heart leaped! There was Ron! She felt her knees turn to water and her stomach knotted.

"Oh, I can't do it, MaryAnn," she whispered and grabbed MaryAnn's arm.

MaryAnn shook her hand off. "Can't do what? Are you crazy? We can't quit now! What's the matter—did you see a ghost?"

"Just look out there!" Jodi said and pointed out Ron. He was chatting with a lady and a man. A little girl crawled up on his lap. "That's Ron! He must be here with his older brother and his family! Oh, MaryAnn, I can't do it!"

"Of course you can. Just grit your teeth and forget that the cutest guy in the country is watching you make a fool of yourself!" MaryAnn chuckled and checked out Ron again.

Jodi's stomach was churning, but she did not have long to feel bad because Mr. Thompson opened the meeting with a few cheery words and then turned it over to them. Jodi avoided looking at Ron.

The skit was about a magician, a banana, and a dummy. Jodi was the dummy, and tried to imitate MaryAnn, who did a trick with a white handkerchief. But Jodi did her trick with a banana and finished the skit with most of it on her face. The audience roared with laughter, and she noticed Ron was laughing, too.

MaryAnn picked up her guitar and introduced the first song while Jodi wiped the banana from her face. They led the group in several folk songs, and then sang a song from Scripture. Jodi let her eyes rest for a few seconds on Ron when he was not looking. The firelight shone on his soft brown hair.

After the singing, Mr. Fong stepped up to them. He was smiling.

"Very good singing," he said. "I wish Susan would learn to play the guitar and sing like that. She is so shy, though."

"How is Susan?" Jodi asked. She let her eyes slide away from Mr. Fong as she glanced toward Ron. He was standing not far away, talking to Mr. Thompson and saying something about only staying tonight.

"—will be fine, I'm sure," Mr. Fong was saying. "And now I want to ask you to come to our cabin and have some tea."

MaryAnn smiled. "Oh, yes, that would be nice. Thank you."

Jodi ran to tell her mother where they were going and to get her purse. On her way back to MaryAnn, she passed Ron. He grinned at her.

"Oh, Jodi," he said. "That was really neat. I didn't know you made such a good dummy!" His brown eyes sparkled with fun.

Jodi felt her face turn red. She laughed self-conciously and flung out her hand in an offhand manner.

"Oh? Didn't you know?" she said, without stopping.

"That's what I do best!" She heard Ron laughing as he turned to go.

Susan was sitting in a chair reading when they came in, but she stood up quickly and went into one of the bedrooms and closed the door.

Mr. Fong shook his head. "My daughter is most unkind. I apologize for her. She is not usually so unfriendly. I am afraid the shock was bad for her the other day."

Jodi waved her hand. "That's OK, Mr. Fong. We understand how she must feel." Mrs. Fong heated some water and poured it into a beautifully painted teapot.

While they were drinking the delicious Chinese tea, Jodi told Mr. Fong how they had found the silver box and the paper inside it. He leaned forward, deeply interested.

"Do you have the paper?" he asked.

Jodi brought her Bible out of her purse and opened it to the maps. She smiled.

"We have reason to believe this may be valuable, so I hid it in the back of my Bible. I do hope you keep this in confidence."

Mr. Fong assured her he would and then leaned over the paper, reading to himself. All was quiet except for the ticking of a clock somewhere in the cabin. Mr. Fong began chuckling.

"What is it?" Jodi asked, intensely curious.

Mr. Fong finished reading and raised his eyes. "This is the legend of the green-eyed dragon," he said with another chuckle.

"That must be the legend of the dragon on the lid of the box!" MaryAnn exclaimed.

"Perhaps," Mr. Fong nodded. "But this story does not seem truly authentic. It is as if someone made it up for his own purposes. I have never heard of such a legend, and I am sure our forefathers would not claim it!"

"What does it say?" Jodi asked.

Mr. Fong sighed. "I will translate roughly what it says. It is hard to put in English—this is the story of five great dragons who ruled the earth. One dragon, who had glittering green eyes, was stronger than the rest and so he ruled everyone. He became puffed up with pride and commanded that everyone worship him."

"Worship a dragon?" MaryAnn asked.

Mr. Fong nodded seriously. "It is done," he said. "And so a great temple was built for this dragon. But the other four dragons were jealous, and so they prepared a trap for the green-eyed dragon. He fell into the trap and injured himself, so he was no longer strong. The five dragons then ruled the world together from then on."

Jodi leaned forward. "Could you tell us what those symbols are that are underlined? We think they might be important."

"Yes, I could do that," Mr. Fong said. "These three here mean pan, but not the kind you would use for cooking. And these two characters mean a temple or shrine—" He paused. "I guess that's all that is underlined. I hope that will help you."

Jodi wrote down the meanings for the characters on the bottom of the paper and then looked up.

"That's really great! Thank you so much for telling us what this means!" She and MaryAnn finished their tea and hurried back down the path through the bushes toward their cabin. It was dark, and they had forgotten their flashlight, so they felt their way along quietly. A mourning dove cooed in the trees above their heads, and they could hear frogs down by the lake. Jodi's thoughts turned to Ron.

Suddenly she stopped. MaryAnn bumped into her and started to say something, but Jodi covered her mouth with her hand.

"Sh!" Jodi whispered. "I think I hear something in

53

those bushes just ahead!" The two girls remained still for a few seconds, listening. Then they heard rustlings in the bushes.

Jodi gulped, her hands sweaty and her knees shaking. "Maybe it's an animal," she whispered.

MaryAnn's cold hand gripped her arm. "Mighty big animal," she whispered back.

Jodi turned to her. "Listen!" she hissed. "Maybe it's Joe, but maybe it's one of the crooks. Take my purse and go back to the office. It's right around that corner. Then go down the path to the lake and follow the beach up to our cabin. I'm going on down the path and find out who's hiding in the bushes!"

MaryAnn shook her head. "Jodi! You can't do that! It's too dangerous. Come with me! Hurry!"

"No!" Jodi took a step down the path. "Get Mom and meet me from the other way. Hurry!" MaryAnn clutched Jodi's purse and stumbled away.

Jodi clenched her teeth to stop them from chattering and took another step toward the bushes that were strangely silent now. Another step. Her eyes stared into the dark depths of the bushes. A twig snapped close by. She whirled toward the sound.

"Who—whoever's in there," she said shakily, "come on out, cuz I know you're there!" She waited and then stepped back as the bushes rustled loudly and then moved. A man pushed them aside and looked at Jodi. He wore a wide-brimmed hat.

Jodi sighed. "Oh, Joe! It's you! Why do you scare me all the time?" The man took a step nearer. She tried to look into his face, but the hat hid most of it. He spoke in a hoarse whisper.

"Sorry, Jodi," he said. "I wanted to see you again."

Jodi laughed, relief sweeping her body. "You could come to the cabin like everyone else. Why are you whispering? There's no one around."

Joe took a step closer. "I changed my mind," he said. "I want that box! Git it for me!" He grabbed her arm.

54

She stepped back, alarmed. Was that liquor on his breath?

"I—I don't have it with me, Joe. Can't you pick it up in the morning? Mom will be wondering where I am."

The grip on her arm tightened. "No, I gotta have it now," he rasped in her face. She recoiled from the foul smell of liquor.

"It's mine, you know. Go git it now! I'll wait here for you, and if you don't bring it, I'll—I'll git the police! Now hurry! And come back with the silver box!" He pushed her down the path. She stumbled, regained her balance, and ran toward the cabin. A few seconds later she saw a beam of light and then her mother and Mary-Ann.

"Jodi!" Mrs. Fischer called. "Are you all right?"

She ran up to them. "I—I guess so. It was Joe. But he wasn't acting normal."

Mrs. Fischer glanced down the dark path. "Joe? At this time of night? And sneaking up on you?" She sighed and shook her head. "Well, come on, we might as well go back."

Later, in the bedroom of the cabin, Jodi and MaryAnn rolled up their sleeping bags and picked up their things. Mrs. Fischer had given them permission to sleep in the motor home, provided they lock the door. Sugar frisked around Jodi's feet, begging for attention.

"What did Joe want?" MaryAnn asked.

Jodi shook her head, sat down on the bed and patted Sugar. "He said he changed his mind and now he wants the silver box. He grabbed my arm and demanded that I bring it to him!" She rubbed her forehead. "I can't understand it. He was drinking, too."

MaryAnn paused and looked at Jodi. "Are you taking him the silver box?"

"No, I don't think so. If he was drinking, he wouldn't be thinking clearly. Maybe he *thinks* he wants it, but from what he said before, he shouldn't have it—I don't know."

MaryAnn picked up her things and tossed her head. "Well, I know," she said. "He's been deceiving us from the very start. Now he's showing his true colors!"

Jodi sighed and picked up her sleeping bag. What could she say? She carried her things outside and shone the light on the door handle while MaryAnn unlocked it. Then she stepped inside and shone the light around.

Jodi gasped. The whole inside of the motor home was one up-turned, dumped-out mess!

6

A Close Call

"MaryAnn!" Jodi called out. "Look!" MaryAnn stepped into the motor home and gasped as Jodi shone the light around. Every drawer was dumped out on the floor. The beds were pulled out and the seats beside the table were lifted.

The closet door was open. "Oh, look!" MaryAnn cried out. "Shine the light over that way. The big mirror on the closet door is smashed. Oh, Mom will be so upset!" She moved inside to inspect the damage, but Jodi stopped her.

"Let's leave things just as they are," she said. "Tomorrow we can call the police and maybe they can find a clue. I'll go tell Mom."

"I'm coming with you!" MaryAnn said and glanced around.

A few seconds later Mrs. Fischer stood in the doorway, taking in the destruction with horror-filled eyes.

"This is awful!" she said. "Who would do such a thing—and why?" She wrapped her robe more tightly around her. "Well, we'll call the police. I've had all the scary things I can take—right up to here!" She hit her forehead.

"I wonder how they got in," Jodi said as they walked back to the cabin. "The door was locked when we came."

Mrs. Fischer shook her head. "No problem for professional thieves. They can pick a lock faster than you can blink your eyes. You girls will have to stay in here tonight." She opened the door of the cabin and turned to face Jodi.

"And you, young lady, can just drop this mystery case, or whatever you call it!"

Jodi gulped. "But, Mom, I just can't—" But Mrs. Fischer had disappeared into her bedroom and firmly shut the door.

A wet tongue, followed by a wiggling body, awoke Jodi the next morning. She pushed Sugar aside and covered her head with the pillow. *If today is anything like yesterday, you can forget it,* she thought.

But then Mrs. Christy's words came back to her. What did she say? Give thanks? Where was it she was reading?

She sat up and reached for her Bible on the suitcase on the floor near her bed. Psalm 139. She read through the psalm and then got up and picked up MaryAnn's *Living Bible* from the table. Verse 14 jumped out at her as she read.

"Thank you for making me—" She closed her eyes and repeated the words, but somehow they did not come from her heart. She sighed.

After a hurried breakfast, they went to the office and Mrs. Fischer told Mr. Thompson about the motor home being ransacked. Before she was finished, Mr. Thompson was on the phone, calling the Royal Canadian Mounted Police office in Wells.

When he hung up he looked at Mrs. Fischer. "The RCMP officers will be out here this afternoon. They're bringing in a specialist in fingerprints. They want you to leave the motor home the way it is." He shook his head. "I sure hope they catch whoever is doing all this."

They walked back to the cabin. Mrs. Fischer took Jodi's hand.

"Jodi," she said quietly, "I'm sorry I got angry with you last night. I know it's not your fault. I just wish you didn't think you had to help this old man."

Jodi smiled. "Oh, Mom. If you knew him, you'd be the first to want to help him. He's really nice—well, sometimes he's nice. But I know he needs help. Everything will turn out all right, I just know it!"

Mrs. Fischer smiled. "I wish I shared your optimism,

58

Jodi," she said.

It was a warm morning, so Jodi and MaryAnn decided to go swimming. Heidi and Heather came, too, swinging their sand buckets and dragging their towels. Sugar bounced excitedly around their feet and then dashed off into the woods to chase a squirrel.

Jodi touched her toe to the water. "Brrr!" she exclaimed, pulling it back out again. The twins splashed into the water and threw some toward Jodi. She screamed and ran back to where MaryAnn was braiding her hair to keep it out of her eyes.

After a quick dip in the lake, the two girls sprawled out on towels in the sun.

"I'd sure like to know what this mystery is all about," MaryAnn said as she unbraided her hair.

Jodi sat cross-legged and watched her. "Well, it must be something someone wants very much. Maybe like a treasure or something."

"That's it, I bet!" MaryAnn cried, her brown eyes sparkling with excitement. "Maybe there's a fabulous cache of gold nuggets that some old miner buried and left behind."

Jodi nodded. "Yeah. And Joe's father knew about it, so he left these clues so Joe could find it when he was gone!" She ran her fingers through her damp curls and sighed. "But why wouldn't Joe take the box when we found it, and why he is so different now?"

MaryAnn was watching something intently out on the lake. She stood up to see it better.

"What are you looking at?" Jodi asked, standing up. MaryAnn pointed. "Look! Just over there!" Jodi saw a dark round object floating on the water.

"Is it a duck?" she asked.

MaryAnn shook her head. "No, I've been watching it for some time. It hasn't moved on its own, only when the water moves. Look! It's closer now!"

Heather pulled on Jodi's arm. "What are you looking at?" she asked.

"I don't know," she said. "Just go play, OK?" And then, in a whisper, she said to MaryAnn, "It looks like a—a head!"

MaryAnn nodded. "That's what I thought! Do you think that's someone's *body*?"

"Oh, what an awful thought!" Jodi shuddered, her mind racing. What if someone had been swimming and drowned out there? Maybe they *just did*! Maybe there was hope! She grabbed MaryAnn.

"I'm going to go out there to find out!" she exclaimed. "It's not very far, and I've taken life-saving classes! Just stay here and be ready for first aid if it *is* someone out there!"

She turned and ran into the water. The icy water took her breath away for a second, but she only paused for a moment to check where the round object was and then started out with strong strokes.

After swimming for a little while, it seemed farther away! Maybe the waves were washing it away now! She began swimming again, but the cold water was beginning to numb her body. Her legs felt tired and her breath was coming in gasps.

The next time she paused, the round thing was closer. It still looked a little like a head, but she was beginning to doubt that it was. Her legs and arms felt like lead. She flipped over in the water to rest, but her body was so cold and tense that she could not float very well. She glanced back and was surprised to see how far she had come.

"Just a little farther," she told herself. She switched to the sidestroke and in a few minutes was close enough to see the round thing clearly. It was a hat! She picked it up out of the water. A wide-brimmed, floppy hat, just like the one Joe wore! Suddenly she wondered what had become of Joe!

Then she turned and, holding the hat in one hand, started back for the shore. But she had come out a long way and the cold was quickly draining her last few reserves of strength. She tried to float on her back and went under. Suddenly, for the first time in her life, she was afraid of the water.

Jodi fought the panic that surged inside. She treaded water for a moment and then tried swimming the side-stroke again. Her legs barely moved in the water, and her head went under again.

This time she was thoroughly frightened. When she came up, she splashed the water and screamed for help. Glancing at the shore, she could see that MaryAnn had made no move to get help. She waved the hat in the air and screamed again.

This time MaryAnn waved back. Jodi let go of the hat, flipped over on her back and swam the backstroke. Her cold, tired muscles responded and she made headway for a few minutes. Then her head went under again.

She swallowed some water and came up spitting. She knew it would not be long before the water won the battle. Waving her hand desperately in the air, she screamed again for help, but the motion caused her head to go under again.

When she blinked the water from her eyes and looked again to the shore, she could see a small figure running along the beach to the resort dock where several boats were tied. MaryAnn had heard her cry for help! She treaded water and tried to relax.

MaryAnn arrived at the dock and climbed into a boat. Someone else was there, too—was it Mr. Thompson? The moments seemed like years to Jodi as she spit water and tried to catch her breath. She was so tired, so very, very tired. It would be so easy just to stop trying, to give in to the pull of the water, close her eyes, and slip away.

Suddenly her eyes blinked open. The water was vibrating with the steady hum of a motor coming closer. She gave a tired kick and saw a boat speeding across the water toward her. MaryAnn sat in the front and Mr. Thompson steered in the back. She waved her hand in the air but the motion caused her to go under the water.

She swallowed some water and came up coughing, gasping for breath. MaryAnn and Mr. Thompson were close now. Mr. Thompson idled the motor and MaryAnn leaned over the side of the boat.

"Jodi! Grab my arms! Here!" She stretched toward Jodi. Jodi grabbed her arms and almost pulled her out of the boat.

Mr. Thompson came closer. "Take it easy, Jodi," he said. "We have you now. Here. I'll lift you into the boat. That'sa girl." She felt herself being lifted by strong arms out of the water. Her mind was whirling, and she kept coughing as Mr. Thompson turned the boat back to the dock.

A few minutes later, Mr. Thompson and some other man lifted her out of the boat and laid her down on the dock. Voices were floating above her. Mrs. Fischer tucked a blanket around her shivering body and leaned over her head.

"Jodi! Can you hear me? Are you all right?" Mrs. Fischer's voice broke.

Jodi coughed again and opened her eyes. "I'm OK," she mumbled. "Just so—cold. Can't get warm." She closed her eyes again.

Then she heard another voice. It was a woman's voice, and seemed full of authority. The woman had everyone stand back. She felt Jodi's pulse, opened her eyelids, and listened to her breathing. Jodi looked up.

A dark-haired lady was leaning over her. The lady looked at Mr. Thompson.

"She's in shock. And suffering from a little exposure. She's swallowed some water. Do you have some coffee?" She tucked someone's T-shirt under Jodi's feet.

Mr. Thompson ran off to his cabin. The lady turned to Mrs. Fischer and MaryAnn.

"Here, you can help. These towels—rub her down good with them. That will get the circulation going."

Oh, it felt so good! The rubbing, anyway. The coffee was like fire. It burned in her mouth, burned all the way

62

down, and the fire grew in her stomach and began warming her body.

She smiled at the dark-haired lady. "Who are you?". she asked. The lady smiled back. "Mrs. Logan. I'm a nurse on vacation. I have a cabin over there." She pointed down the lake. "I was just over for some gas when I saw the commotion on the beach."

"Well, you were certainly an answer to prayer," Mrs. Fischer commented and paused from rubbing Jodi's leg. She looked at her. "Feel like going home yet?"

Jodi nodded and sat up. Suddenly everything whirled in a dizzy circle. Mrs. Logan laid her hand on her shoulder.

"Easy does it, Jodi," she said. "And I want you to rest today, OK?" She patted Jodi and stood up.

Mr. Thompson smiled at Mrs. Logan. "Thank you so much for your help," he said. Then he turned to Jodi.

"I guess you don't need a lecture, but I do want to say that it was the cold water that drained your strength so quickly. This lake is known for its icy water. Well, I hope you're feeling better, and take it easy." He turned and walked back to the office.

Jodi shook her head. "I feel so dumb. Just the kind of thing they warned us about in life-saving classes. But I guess I didn't think. I just wanted to get out there—" She paused.

Mrs. Fischer helped her to her feet and Jodi leaned on her and MaryAnn as they walked along the beach back to the cabin.

"What in the world made you swim out there like that?" Mrs. Fischer asked after a bit.

MaryAnn was carrying something wet and floppy. She held it up. "This!" she said.

Mrs. Fischer stopped to look at the hat, and the twins crowded close. She turned to Jodi.

"I still don't understand," she said. "Suppose you start at the first and tell me what happened."

Jodi sighed and began relating what had just happened. When she finished they had arrived at the beach below the cabin. Jodi decided to rest on the towels in the sun, and Mrs. Fischer went up to the cabin to fix lunch. Sugar greeted them with short, excited barks, and then licked Jodi's face.

"Wonder whose hat that is," MaryAnn said after a while. Jodi turned her head so she could see the hat where MaryAnn had placed it carefully over a rock to dry.

"I bet it's Joe's," she said slowly. "It looks just like the one he always wears."

"But why would he throw his hat into the water?" MaryAnn asked. She watched a boat out on the lake.

Jodi raised herself to one elbow, the sparkle returning to her blue eyes.

"Maybe he's in trouble!" she said suddenly. "So he threw his hat in the water and hoped it would float over this way, and we would see it and come and help him!"

MaryAnn stood up and stared at the boat that was swiftly approaching. "Speaking of Joe," she said slowly.

Jodi whirled around and then sprang to her feet. The world spun around in a big, dizzy circle and she grabbed MaryAnn's arm.

"Still—a little—dizzy," she said. She regained her balance and focused her eyes on the boat. It was green, and in the back was a little man with a wide-brimmed hat.

About ten feet from the shore, he cut the motor and the boat drifted up to the gravelly beach. He jumped out nimbly and pulled the boat closer. Then he turned to the girls.

"Joe!" Jodi exclaimed. The little old man looped his thumbs behind his suspenders and grinned.

"Howdy," he said. "Just come acallin' to see how you girls are makin' out. Also, to find out if you still had ahold of that there silver box of mine."

MaryAnn nodded. "Yes, we do. It's hidden in the—"

Jodi squeezed her arm. "In a very good place," she finished.

Joe nodded. He reached into his pocket and pulled out a box of cigarettes and lit one. Then he glanced at Jodi, and his brown eyes glittered with greed.

"In the *what*?" he asked. "Just where is it hidden?" He puffed out a cloud of blue smoke.

Jodi did not answer right away. Instead she strolled down to the boat Joe had come in. She glanced at the sides to see if there was a name on it, but there was none. Then she looked in the boat and jumped as if she were stung! A rifle lay in the bottom of the boat! Maybe it was the one that had shot at them!

"Now, you just stay away from that there boat," Joe suddenly exclaimed and stepped over to Jodi. He grabbed her arm and turned her around. She leaned against the boat.

"Where is the box?" Joe asked again, sneering into her face. His grip tightened on her arm.

"I—I can't—" Up above them the cabin door slammed shut. Jodi paused to listen. A few seconds later, Heidi was running down the path.

"Jodi!" she called. "Mom says to come right away! Those police officers are here and they want to talk to you!"

A shock coursed through Joe's body. He dropped Jodi's arm, pushed the boat into the water, leaped into it, and roared away.

Jodi sighed with relief and then turned to run up the path. But she got dizzy again, so she paused and glanced out on the lake. The boat was going around the point in the direction of the cabin!

She turned to walk slowly up the path. Why had Joe changed so much? Did his experience with Jesus Christ not mean anything to him?

Officer Davis was standing beside the motor home talking with Mrs. Fischer when Jodi came up by the cabin.

"Oh, here she is," Mrs. Fischer said. "I was just telling Officer Davis about your close call in the lake just now, Jodi. But I don't suppose you want to talk about it."

Jodi blushed and grinned. "No, I don't. Have you gotten any fingerprints yet?" She stepped up to the motor home and looked in the open door.

A policeman was leaning over the table, sprinkling some kind of dust on it.

"This is Officer Edwards," Officer Davis said. "He's our specialty man from Kamloops. How is it going, Edwards? Got any clear prints yet?"

Officer Edwards lifted his dark head. "No, I'm afraid not. Looks like a pro job. Must have worn gloves. I'll keep trying, though. Maybe I'll get lucky and find some."

Mrs. Fischer invited Officer Davis to the porch of the cabin where she served sandwiches and iced tea. Jodi, MaryAnn, and the wide-eyed twins found places to sit while Sugar frisked between them, begging for handouts.

Jodi turned to Officer Davis. "Have you had any success in finding the man who shot at us?" she asked.

Officer Davis shook his blond head and frowned. "No, we haven't. We are going to spend some time today inquiring at the various cabins and resorts along the lake. Also, we've had a report of a stolen boat from the Green Haven Resort. You haven't seen any stray green boats, have you?"

Jodi choked on her iced tea and glanced at MaryAnn. MaryAnn's face was pale and her brown eyes were wide.

"Well, yes, we have, sort of," Jodi replied.

Mrs. Fischer turned to her. "Would you pour some more iced tea first, Jodi?" she asked.

Jodi stood up in a daze and started for the cabin door. Suddenly she heard a gasp behind her. She whirled around. Everyone was staring at her! MaryAnn pointed her finger toward her.

"Jodi!" she said in a strangled whisper. "You have *green paint* all over you!"

7

A Hidden Message

Officer Davis cleared his throat. "I—I don't want to embarrass you, Jodi, but I must ask where you saw a green boat recently and how you came to have green paint on yourself."

Jodi looked at the back of her legs, and saw big splotches of green paint. She sat down weakly.

"I—I don't know where I got the paint," she said slowly, her mind spinning. Mrs. Fischer shook her head and went to get the iced tea.

MaryAnn pushed back her long, dark hair. "We can tell you where we saw the green boat. It was pulled up here on the beach not ten minutes ago!" She pointed dramatically toward the lake and the twins gasped. The policeman jumped to his feet and stared out to the lake. He turned back to Jodi.

"Do you know who it belongs to?" he asked.

She shook her head. "An old man was driving it, but it didn't have any name on it. I looked to be sure. That's when I saw the rifle in the bottom of the boat! And then Joe pushed me back against the boat—hey! That's where I got the green paint!"

Officer Davis nodded. "Yes, the thieves have painted over the words with green paint. The boat was the stolen one. Who is this old man and what can you tell me about him?"

"Well, his name is Joe, or Sucker Joe. I never heard his last name," Jodi began. She and MaryAnn told the policeman all that had happened. When they finished, Jodi stood up.

"I'll go get the silver box," she said. "You can have the address book we found and the scribbled note." She ran to the motor home and explained to Officer Edwards

67

that she needed the hammer. He found it for her, and she soon returned to the cabin with the precious silver box in her hands.

Officer Davis and the others looked at it closely. Then he took the address book and the note and slipped them into his pocket.

"You keep this," he said and handed the box back to Jodi. "I can see why someone might want to steal it if they saw it, but this case seems more involved than that. I want you girls to keep your eyes open. You may find out more than we can. In the meantime, I'm going to pay this Joe character a visit!"

Back at the motor home, Officer Edwards met them with a smile.

"I found a set of clear prints!" he exclaimed. "Let's get going! I'd like to see if this fellow has a record."

After the officers left, Jodi removed the green paint from her legs with MaryAnn's fingernail polish remover, and then changed into her jeans and a T-shirt. Sitting on the porch with a magazine while MaryAnn and Mrs. Fischer cleaned up the motor home, Jodi found her thoughts going back to Joe.

Was it worth helping someone so mean? Someone who might be deceiving them and in trouble with the law? Then she remembered when she had first met him—his warm-hearted friendliness, his troubled eyes, and his openness to the Savior.

"How are you feeling, Jodi?" Mrs. Fischer asked after a little while. She went into the cabin and settled down with a book.

Jodi smiled, her blue eyes sparkling. "Great, Mom! Just like ever. In fact, I was wondering if we could take the boat out for a little bit."

Her mother's eyebrows came down. "Jodi, you heard the nurse. You're supposed to rest today."

"But, Mom, I feel really good!" Jodi replied with her head tilted and her blue eyes pleading. "It doesn't take

68

much strength to steer a motorboat. Please, Mom? Just for a short ride?"

Mrs. Fischer shook her head and sighed. "Oh, Jodi, I get tired just watching you go. Go ahead, but you better not be gone long! Is that clear?"

Jodi and MaryAnn bolted for the door.

"And slow down!" Mrs. Fischer called from inside the cabin.

Jodi giggled as they walked to the boats.

"Poor Mom," she said. "She says I give her all her gray hairs!"

"Speaking of gray hairs," MaryAnn commented. "This case sure doesn't look good for Joe. I think we should forget trying to help him."

Jodi turned to MaryAnn. "You've got it all wrong! Joe is in trouble. I know he needs our help! We should still love him even if he isn't nice all the time."

Mr. Thompson glanced up from a boat he was painting bright blue.

"Hi, girls. Feeling better already, Jodi?"

Jodi nodded. "Just like ever," she said. "We'd like to take a boat out for a little bit."

Mr. Thompson nodded. "I fixed that one you took the other day. Don't be gone too long, though, it looks like a storm is coming up."

Jodi glanced up. Huge, black clouds were forming over the lake. A brisk breeze fanned her face.

Hurriedly they launched the boat and in a short while were skimming over the waves on the lake. Jodi enjoyed the breeze and the fine spray of water from the prow of the boat. She pointed the boat toward the Green Haven Resort. Soon they rounded a point of land and saw it snuggled in its bay.

When they were close to the dock, she cut the motor and coasted in. MaryAnn jumped out and tied up the boat.

"Listen," Jodi whispered when she had stepped on

69

the dock. "I want to look around, unnoticed. Look, right up there through the trees is the office. You go and strike up a conversation with the person in there. I'll look around. Meet me back here in ten minutes, OK?"

MaryAnn stepped back. "If we're doing this for Joe, I don't know if I want to be a part of it," she said out loud.

But Jodi checked her watch, patted MaryAnn on the arm, and trotted to the cover of some trees along the beach. From there she followed the paths to several cabins and poked around some of the buildings. She was just about to return to the boat when something shiny caught her eye in the bushes. A small, unused road led into the bushes, and there she found Joe's blue Volkswagen!

"This is it!" she whispered to herself. "I'm sure of it. Now, why would he park it in here, hidden from anyone seeing it? Hm, I wonder."

She turned and ran back to the beach and walked out on the dock toward their boat. Hearing voices behind her, she turned to see MaryAnn hurrying toward her with a fat, bald man following.

The bald man spotted Jodi, and a smile spread across his face.

"Oh, I see there's two of you," he chortled loudly. His face was flushed and Jodi could see he had been drinking. "Now, that's real nice—two pretty, young girls come to visit. You don't have to hurry away, you know. Stay and have some tea—or a beer," He laughed loudly.

MaryAnn began running, her face white and her dark hair streaming out behind her. She reached Jodi and grabbed her arm.

"Let's get out of here!" she panted. "He's crazy and drunk!"

Jodi leaped into the boat and MaryAnn untied it and

climbed in. In her hurry, Jodi pulled the rope wrong and the motor only sputtered and then died. The bald man wheezed out onto the dock and grabbed the prow of the boat.

"Like I said—" He leered at them. "Stay with me. You'll be all right. I can take care of two young girls!" He put his head back and laughed.

Jodi yanked hard on the rope again and the motor roared to life. She crammed the lever to full speed and the boat lurched away from the dock, pulling the man into the water. He began splashing and sputtering.

"Think we should go back?" MaryAnn hollered over the noise of the motor.

Jodi glanced back. "No, he has hold of the dock already." She grinned. "Might help sober him up some, anyway!"

MaryAnn shook her head. *"You* can laugh! I'm the one who had to go in and talk to the nut! So help me, Jodi, I'm never covering for you again!"

The boat rounded a point of land and Jodi cut the speed. She shook her head.

"It's my fault, MaryAnn. But I never guessed there would be someone like him there!" she said. "If it makes you feel better, I did find something important."

"Well, I certainly hope so after all that!"

Jodi grinned. MaryAnn's bark was worse than her bite.

"I found Joe's car!" she said.

MaryAnn blinked. "Was it lost?"

"No, not that I know of," Jodi replied. "But it was sort of hidden away behind some bushes, as if someone didn't want it seen."

MaryAnn shook her head. "This is getting worse. Why would Joe want to park his car in the bushes at the Green Haven Resort?"

The boat rounded another point of land, and Jodi suddenly cut the motor off. They were fairly close to

71

shore and she could see the old, deserted cabin where she had seen the man's face before. The boat drifted silently up to the beach.

"What in the world—" MaryAnn asked, cross and puzzled. "Sh!" Jodi hissed. "I want to look around! We have to be very quiet!"

MaryAnn pushed back her long hair. "Well, you go. I'm staying right here this time," she whispered.

Jodi rolled up her jeans, jumped out into the knee-deep water, and pulled the boat in closer to shore. She paused for a moment beside the boat.

"Just hurry!" MaryAnn whispered. "The wind's picking up!"

Jodi glanced up. The clouds were rolling in like giant puffs of black cotton. If she did not hurry, they would not make it back before the storm struck. She ran up the beach, her shoes sloshing water, and hid in the bushes.

A few minutes later she heard a door slam. Men's voices drifted down to her hiding place, but she could not make out what they were saying. She shivered as the wind bit through her T-shirt. What were those men doing here? Did the cabin belong to them?

Then she heard a truck start up and roar away. Once again the woods were silent except for the wind in the trees. She crept toward the cabin.

Suddenly she stopped. Right in front of her was a big pile of brush. As she looked for a way around, something green caught her eye. She shoved some of the brush aside and was surprised that it was thrown loosely over something at the bottom. Some more branches and sticks went flying down, and then she stopped. Her blue eyes were wide with amazement.

A green boat was hidden here! She shoved more branches off the boat and looked at it. Yes, the green paint was sticky on one side.

"The stolen boat!" she whispered to herself. "Now, I wonder who those men were?" She glanced up to the cabin. Did she dare go up and look around?

72

She glanced at MaryAnn waiting on the beach. Mary-Ann motioned frantically for her to come. The wind was whipping the lake into frothy whitecaps. She hesitated for a second and then turned back to the cabin.

Just one quick look around! Watching the dark windows on the cabin, she slowly crept nearer. Was there someone in the dark watching her every move? She circled behind the cabin and saw a woodpile with freshly cut wood, bark, and sticks lying around. There was garbage and she saw fresh tracks in the dirt. She walked around quietly, keeping an eye on the back door.

She glanced around once more and then turned to go to the beach. But suddenly she stopped. What was that in the dirt? At first it looked like chicken scratching. She knelt down. They were letters, partly rubbed out by a footprint!

She traced the first letter with her finger. It was an *H*. The second and third letters were partly ruined, but the fourth was a *P*. She looked again at the third letter. It was a straight line down. Was it an *L*? The second letter was almost gone, but she made out a straight line down.

She sat back on her heels. Was it a message? What did it mean? She studied the letters again. Suddenly the meaning struck her!

Of course! *The word was HELP!*

8

An Important Clue

A twig snapped, and Jodi leaped to her feet and whirled around. It was MaryAnn, standing at the bottom of the hill near the beach. Her face was white and drawn. Jodi ran down to her.

"Jodi! Look! The storm's here!" MaryAnn whispered. Jodi became aware of the rain that was pelting down and the waves that were smashing against the beach.

She shook her head. "We can't use the boat now," she said.

"How are we getting home, then?" MaryAnn wailed. "You and your crazy ideas!" They were both becoming drenched.

Jodi felt as though someone had slapped her. She blinked her long lashes to keep back the tears and turned to the beach. She yanked the boat high up on the sand and then turned to MaryAnn.

"I don't know why you hang around me, MaryAnn!" she said angrily. "I'm always getting you in trouble!"

MaryAnn grabbed her arm. "Oh, Jodi, stop! I'm just scared! How are we getting home?"

Jodi looked at MaryAnn and suddenly felt sorry for her. She put her arm around MaryAnn's soggy shoulders.

"Well, there's a road that winds around the lake, and it will take us back to the resort. Buck up, old girl—it's probably only two or three miles!"

Jodi led the way around the cabin and showed MaryAnn where she had seen the message. The rain was washing it away. Then they walked down the driveway and out to the road.

"Guess what," Jodi said. "I found that stolen boat, too!"

MaryAnn stopped, her brown eyes big. "You found it? Where?"

"It was right near the beach, covered with a big pile of branches and stuff." They sloshed down the narrow, winding road.

MaryAnn shook her head. "What does it all mean? A stolen boat, a message for help scrawled in the dirt, Joe's car tucked away in the bushes."

"And before I found the boat," Jodi put in, "I heard some men talking behind the cabin, and then they left in a truck. A real noisy truck."

"I think I heard it, too." MaryAnn nodded. "Who do you think it was?"

"It sounded an awful lot like the truck that those men were driving at our resort. You know, the big fat man and the little skinny one that followed us in Barkerville."

"Hey!" MaryAnn yelled suddenly. "Get over! I think I hear a car coming!" They looked back and saw a red sports car coming at them at high speed. Suddenly Jodi realized that the driver was not getting over for them! She screamed and leaped into the ditch, pulling MaryAnn with her. As the car whizzed past, she saw a fat, bald man behind the wheel.

"Whew! That was close," MaryAnn said as they picked themselves up.

Jodi looked down the road, her face white and her heart pounding.

"That wasn't an accident, MaryAnn!" she exclaimed. "That was Old Baldy from the Green Haven! He saw us in enough time to get over. He just didn't want to!"

"Nice guy," MaryAnn commented sarcastically.

It was much later, and although the rain had let up some, Jodi and MaryAnn were very wet when they turned down the driveway into the Bowron Lakes Resort. Mr. Thompson and Mrs. Fischer were just coming up from the beach.

"Mom! We're back!" Jodi called.

75

Mrs. Fischer looked up and relief flooded her face. Mr. Thompson frowned.

"We thought you might have been lost at sea," he said, his voice a little uneven. "What happened?"

Jodi gulped. "Well, I stopped to look at something and the storm came up so quickly. We had to walk home."

MaryAnn sneezed.

"Where's the boat, Jodi?" Mr. Thompson asked wearily. "I'll have to go get it."

"Just down the road there's an old cabin. Next place. I don't think anyone's there. The boat is on the beach. I'm sorry, Mr. Thompson."

He waved his hand and turned to go.

"And I found that stolen boat, too!" Jodi exclaimed. "I should call the police."

"You can use the phone in the office," Mr. Thompson said and began running to his truck.

Mrs. Fischer took hold of Jodi's arm. "Not before you two come out of this rain and get dry clothes on," she said firmly.

Mrs. Fischer said very little as she hurried the girls to the cabin, had them change into dry clothes, and heated some hot chocolate. Her mouth was held in a firm, tight line, and Jodi knew she had pressed her good nature too far.

MaryAnn was coming down with a cold, so Mrs. Fischer tucked her into the big overstuffed chair and gave her an aspirin and some vitamin C tablets.

Jodi sipped her hot chocolate and absent-mindedly patted Sugar. She glanced at her mother.

"Mom, it wasn't our fault, really. That storm came up so fast. We went down to the Green Haven Resort, which isn't very far, and then stopped once more on the way back. That's all."

Mrs. Fischer turned to her. "I know, Jodi. It's *never* your fault. But, just the same, you get into all kinds of trouble. I think until your father gets back, you two are going to stay around this cabin and catch up on some reading and letter writing."

Jodi groaned. "Oh, Mom, that sounds like school! This is supposed to be our vacation. How can we have fun sitting around?"

"It's supposed to be *my* vacation, too, you know," Mrs. Fischer replied, a smile easing the worry in her voice. "And I know I'll enjoy it a lot more if you two are here where I can keep an eye on you."

Jodi finished her drink and slipped on her jacket. "Well, I have to go call the police, Mom. I have to report finding that stolen boat."

Mrs. Fischer put her coat on. "I'll come along just to make sure you don't get into trouble."

In the resort office, Jodi dialed the RCMP detachment in Wells.

"Hello," she said to the secretary. "This is Jodi Fischer. I'm staying at the Bowron Lakes Resort, and I'd like to report finding what may be the stolen boat that was reported earlier today . . . Yes, about two miles past this resort, there's an old cabin. The boat is hidden in some bushes near the water's edge below the cabin . . . Yes . . . OK. Good-bye." She hung up the phone and turned to her mother.

"Officer Davis and the other officer are still out here, so she said she would radio them and tell them what I found."

Her mother sighed. "Well, I'm glad that's over with. Now back to the cabin with you!"

After supper, the rain let up, so Mrs. Fischer and the twins took Sugar for a short walk along the beach. Jodi stayed with MaryAnn. She sat at the table, trying to write a letter.

"Oh, MaryAnn!" she exclaimed and threw down her pen. "This is impossible! I can't concentrate on this letter. I keep trying to figure out this mystery. Everything seems so confused!"

MaryAnn nodded. "I know what you mean. Hey!

77

Why don't we write some more down, like we did before. I'll go get that tablet." She pulled on her sweater and ran out to the motor home.

"Read what we have so far," Jodi said and leaned back in her chair. "There is something important that we've missed—I'm sure of it!"

She listened with half-closed eyes as MaryAnn read of the mystery up to the time when the man shot at them from the boat. Suddenly she leaned forward, her chair banging against the floor.

"Hey, maybe that man who shot at us is the same one who stole the boat," she said. "And he had a wide-brimmed hat on like Joe wears."

MaryAnn nodded. "But let's get back to the things that have happened. First, the boat motor was tampered with, and you think you saw a face in the window of the cabin."

Jodi frowned. "Think! I know I did. And what's more, I bet that's the man who stole the boat and shot at us. He must be the one who got into the motor home. He must know more about this mystery than we do!"

MaryAnn waved her hand. "Slow down. I can't write that fast." She scribbled away, and then looked up. "Now what?"

Jodi frowned in thought. "Now we have the strange behavior of Joe—"

"Wait a minute," MaryAnn countered. "How can you say his behavior is strange, when you hardly know him? You don't really know how he acts normally."

Jodi nodded. "That's right, but you see, there's something in *here*," and she patted her heart, "that tells me Joe doesn't normally act mean."

"Facts!" MaryAnn said. "We need facts, Jodi. A detective has to go on facts, not on feelings!" She thumped the table.

"No, that's where you're wrong," Jodi said and stood up. "Sometimes the toughest cases have been solved by *hunches*. Feelings. And I know something is funny about Joe—" She paused, deep in thought. There *was* something funny about Joe. What was it?

Her mind went back to the scenes of her meetings with Joe. Something inside told her she must remember what it was. The whole mystery hung in the balance. She closed her eyes. The thought was there, it was only playing hide and seek in the memory corridors of her mind. There! She had it! She whirled to MaryAnn.

"I know—" She paused. Heavy footsteps thudded on the porch, and a second later someone was knocking at the door.

Jodi looked at MaryAnn and swallowed. She looked at the door.

"Who—who's there?" she asked.

"Officer Davis," came the deep reply. Jodi sighed with relief and opened the door. The two police officers stepped inside.

"Just came to let you know what happened," Officer Davis said. "We went to that cabin and searched up and down the beach for the boat, Jodi, but we couldn't find it anywhere."

Jodi gasped. "But it was there this afternoon! I bet someone came and moved it. Oh, dear, it's my fault, too. I didn't pile the branches back on it, and they could tell someone had found it!"

Officer Davis waved his hand. "That's OK. We did see where the boat was pulled out of the bushes, and we got several pictures of their foot-prints. We also got some clear fingerprints from the doorknob of the cabin. I suspect that this person is the same one who shot at you." He paused. "Now, about this Joe. We visited his cabin in Barkerville, but he hasn't been there for several days. No one has seen him anywhere. Even his car vanished."

"Oh!" Jodi exclaimed. "I saw his car! It was this afternoon. At the Green Haven Resort. It was pulled off the driveway into some bushes, as if someone wanted to hide it." She paused for breath.

"Yeah, and a man was there who was very rude and tried to keep us there," MaryAnn put in. "And later he tried to run us off the road!"

Officer Davis shook his head. "Sounds like the hired man. Maybe he knows more than he's saying. We'll go back there and take a look around before going home." He paused. "Now, you girls be careful! There is a gang of professional crooks out here. Stay in touch, OK?"

The next day was cloudy and dark. Jodi and Mary-Ann stayed close to the cabin. When Mrs. Fischer went outside for a moment, Jodi turned to MaryAnn.

"Do you realize that today is Thursday and we're getting nowhere on this mystery?" she said anxiously. "Dad is coming back Saturday and we'll be going home!"

"So what?" MaryAnn asked. "It'll be great to get home. Mom said we could go shopping for some school clothes, and—"

"MaryAnn!" Jodi burst out. "What about this mystery and helping Joe? He said his birthday was on Saturday! I have the feeling that something important is going to happen before then!"

MaryAnn sneezed. "Sure, there is. The men are coming back, and we're going home!" She began reading.

Jodi turned and stomped out on the porch. *Some friend! She doesn't even care! But if I wasn't such a dumb-dumb, I'd have this mystery solved by now. All I do is keep getting in trouble. My mother can't even trust me out of her sight!*

She heard a rustling of bushes down the path and looked up. Mrs. Christy was coming toward her. Sugar began barking, so Jodi picked her up. She frowned.

Mrs. Christy smiled. "It's so nice to see you, Jodi! I wanted to come by and say good-bye. I'm leaving for home in a few minutes. Is your mother here?"

Jodi shook her head. "She went somewhere. She'll be back in a few minutes. Want to come in?"

Mrs. Christy shook her head, concern creeping into her sparkly brown eyes.

"No, I really can't," she said and paused. "I've been praying for you, Jodi. How have things been going?"

"Pretty good," Jodi replied and looked down at Sugar.

Mrs. Christy stepped up on the porch and laid her hand lightly on Jodi's arm.

"Something tells me things aren't so good," she said softly. "Have you gotten it right with the Lord, Jodi? Have you thanked Him for the way He made you and resolved to accept yourself?"

Jodi shook her head. "No, not really." She sighed. "I guess I should."

"Yes, you should. Today," Mrs. Christy replied. Then she dug through her purse. "The Fongs were leaving just a moment ago, and I mentioned I was coming here to tell you folks good-bye." She paused and pulled out a small white envelope.

"Here it is! That Chinese girl—what's her name? Susan? She gave this to me and said to give it to you. It was funny, too. She seemed so nervous and frightened—anyway, here it is." Mrs. Christy handed the envelope to Jodi. On the outside was scrawled, "Jodi." She slipped it into her pocket.

Just then Mrs. Fischer came up onto the porch. They exchanged addresses and invitations, and told Mrs. Christy good-bye.

"She is a very exceptional woman," Mrs. Fischer commented as she started lunch. "Here, Jodi, you can put these things on the table. Now, where is Heather?"

Suddenly Jodi heard Sugar barking furiously out in the woods. She froze as she heard a scream. Mrs. Fischer looked up, her face pale.

"Was that Heather?" she asked.

Jodi felt numb. "She just went out—I think to the outhouse."

Mrs. Fischer dropped a handful of knives and bolted for the door. Jodi, MaryAnn, and Heidi followed her.

"Heather!" Mrs. Fischer called. "Where are you?" They ran down the path and then stopped abruptly. Heather was sobbing and running down the path toward them.

Mrs. Fischer scooped her up in her arms and held her close. She was sobbing hysterically. They carried her back to the cabin.

Jodi's mother laid her on the couch and sponged off her face with a facecloth.

"It's OK now, honey," she said and stroked her brown hair. "Can you tell me what frightened you?"

"Oh, Mom! It was awful! It was this man. A big, fat man with a beard." Heather began sobbing again and Mrs. Fischer patted her. Jodi looked at MaryAnn.

"What did he want, Heather?" Jodi asked.

Heather sniffed. "He—he grabbed me from the bushes. That's when Sugar started barking and I screamed. He said he wanted me to get a silver box for him. I said I didn't know where it was, and he squeezed my arm." She began crying again.

"And that's when he heard us and disappeared back into the woods," Jodi continued. Heather nodded.

"That's OK," Mrs. Fischer said. "We won't talk about it anymore. He's gone now, and we won't let anything happen to you. OK?" She stood up and motioned for Jodi to follow her out to the porch.

"Jodi," she said, her blue eyes snapping. "This is it. I'm not taking any more. We're going to get packed up and go home."

Jodi gulped. "Right now?"

"Right now. On the way through Wells, you can drop off that silver box and whatever else you have at the RCMP office. That's final. Now let's get busy!"

Jodi caught her arm. "But, Mom! Dad and Mr. Laine will be coming back soon. How will they get home?"

Mrs. Fischer paused. "Well, I'll just have to come back for them in our car." She went into the cabin and finished making lunch.

Jodi was so miserable she could hardly eat. She knew her mother's mind was made up and nothing would change it now. She washed the dishes and then went to the bedroom to roll up her sleeping bag and pack her suitcase. MaryAnn laid her hand on her shoulder.

"Jodi, I'm sorry this happened—" She paused. "I really do care about Joe, and I wish we could help him."

Jodi shrugged off her hand. "Well, it doesn't matter now." She plopped down on the bed. "Just when I almost had this mystery figured out. You know, before Officer Davis came last night, I thought of something really important, but I can't remember it now!"

Suddenly she sat up straight. "Oh! I almost forgot! Mrs. Christy gave me this note from Susan Fong!" She drew out the small, white envelope from her pocket. "I wonder what it says."

Tearing it open, she took out a single piece of white paper. "Jodi and MaryAnn," she read, while MaryAnn leaned over her shoulder. "I am so sorry I acted so impolite the evening you came to our cabin. I am so frightened. The day we were shot at, I went to get water at the lake and a man came out of the bushes. He told me to find out where you hid that silver box! I just ran back to the cabin. We have decided to go home. I can't stand this place. Maybe the next time we meet it will be under better circumstances. Your friend, Susan Fong."

MaryAnn whistled. "Wow! No wonder she was scared! I wonder what the man who came at her looked like."

"I don't know." Jodi sighed. "And I guess it doesn't matter anyway!" She tore up the note and then stood and finished rolling up her sleeping bag.

Mrs. Fischer looked in. "Will you girls straighten things up in the motor home?" she asked. "Not much to do since we haven't used it, but make sure everything is put away. And get that silver box, Jodi."

Jodi and MaryAnn put on their sweaters and walked

to the motor home. Jodi glanced at the sky and shivered. The clouds were still low and black. A wind was moaning in the treetops. MaryAnn unlocked the motor home and got a hammer for Jodi. Jodi went down the path to the outhouse.

Calling Sugar, she peered into the bushes. Was the fat man still hiding, waiting for her to come along? Goose bumps rose on her arms. Sugar bounced into the woods on the trail of a squirrel.

Before she went in, she circled the outhouse and walked a little way into the woods on each side. No one was around. She went in and pried the board loose with the hammer. The nails screeched as she worked. She paused. Did she just imagine hearing a step nearby? The goose bumps raced down her back and a cold sweat came out on her forehead. Where was Sugar?

She pulled the board away from the wall and reached in to get the box. Her fingers touched something solid. Pulling it up, she laid the box on the seat and then hammered the board in again. Then she tucked the box under her blouse, whistled for Sugar, and ran to the motor home.

"Whew!" she exclaimed. "That was scary! Should I put it under the seat again?"

MaryAnn nodded. "I don't see why not. The crooks have already searched in here. They wouldn't come back." Jodi put the box under the seat and then she and MaryAnn stepped outside.

She turned back to the cabin with a heavy heart. If there were only some way she could stay and solve this mystery and help Joe!

Oh, God, she prayed silently. *Please help! Make it possible for me to help Joe.*

Suddenly she heard voices. She glanced up and stared out to the lake. There! A canoe! Somebody calling and waving!

MaryAnn waved and ran down the path to the beach

with Sugar barking behind her. Jodi turned toward the cabin.

"Mom! Mom!" she yelled. "They're back! Dad and Mr. Laine!" Mrs. Fischer stepped out onto the porch with a worried look on her pretty face.

"What's the matter, now, Jodi?" she asked.

"Look!" Jodi pointed to the beach where the men were just pulling up in the canoe. "The men are back!"

A big smile swept across Mrs. Fischer's face. "Thank goodness!" she said softly, and began running to the beach.

Mr. Fischer and Mr. Laine had grubby beards, and Brian's face was dirty, but to Jodi they were the most beautiful people in the world.

"Man, am I hungry for a solid meal!" Mr. Fischer exclaimed as everyone packed gear up to the cabin. "I hope you saved something good for tonight!"

He pushed the cabin door open and looked around in surprise. "Hey, you have everything packed!"

Mrs. Fischer nodded. "I was going to leave tonight. Things have been really bad with this mystery Jodi's working on. I couldn't take it any more. I was going to come back Saturday to pick you up."

Mr. Fischer rubbed his forehead and sat down. "Well, I'm glad we got back when we did. We're famished, and tired. I think we can stick it out for tonight anyway. Let's stay tonight and get an early start for home tomorrow."

Jodi felt like shouting, jumping, and kissing everyone. But she only gave Brian a quick hug and flashed a big smile to MaryAnn. Inwardly, she thanked the Lord for hearing and answering her prayer.

Mrs. Fischer began fixing another lunch and Jodi and MaryAnn asked for permission to take a walk. After Brian finished a sandwich and a piece of cake, he joined them at the beach with Sugar at his heels.

"What's been happening that's got Mom on her high

horse?" he asked. Jodi told him of being shot at and how Joe had changed. Then they told him about the legend of the green-eyed dragon.

"Go get my purse, Brian, and I'll show you what those underlined symbols mean," Jodi said excitedly. "And take this dumb dog with you back to the cabin. I can't chase after her."

When Brian returned, swinging Jodi's purse, she took out her Bible and showed him the meanings of the Chinese characters. Glancing nervously around, she shut the book.

"C'mon," she said and started down the beach. "I've been cooped up for so long, I've gotta get out!"

As they went, Jodi and MaryAnn told Brian everything else that had happened since he left. Jodi ran her fingers through her hair.

"And there's something I thought of last night that would help solve everything," she said. "But I forgot it—let's see, it was about Joe. And there was something funny about him recently—"

Brian picked up a rock. "Tell me more about him. I mean, after he changed."

MaryAnn thought a minute. "Well, the time I saw him, he drove up to our beach in this green boat. He was wearing that wide-brimmed hat he always does—"

"Hey!" Brian exclaimed. "You said you had just fished it out of the lake! Did he ask for his old one back?"

Jodi shook her head. "No, he didn't. I just thought he must have two hats. But, that does seem unlikely."

MaryAnn continued. "He wore old jeans and suspenders, and he took a cigarette from his pocket and lit it—"

"Hey! The cigarette!" Jodi exclaimed suddenly. "Before, when I was at his cabin, he rolled his own! Now he has boughten ones! Don't you think that's strange?"

Brian nodded. "Yeah. Is there anything else?" He stepped over a log that had been washed up on shore.

86

Jodi thought. "Yes, there was. He wanted to know where the box was hidden. When I didn't tell him, he became very angry. He marched over to me and grabbed my arm. And his eyes! They were dark and angry!"

She stopped suddenly and swung around. "That's it! I just remembered it!"

"What? What is it?" MaryAnn asked.

"The thing I thought of last night and couldn't remember!" she exclaimed. "Joe's eyes! They were brown yesterday—before, they were *blue*!"

9

Joe Tells His Story

MaryAnn stared at Jodi, her brown eyes wide. "What—what does that mean, Jodi?" she asked.

Jodi swallowed hard. Her heart was beating double-time, and she found it hard to breathe.

"Well," she began. "You can't change the color of your eyes. It seems that someone has been impersonating Joe!"

MaryAnn gasped. "But—but he looks exactly like Joe!"

"There *were* differences, though," Jodi replied. "Now that I think of it, this other man looked younger, and thinner, too."

"But where does that leave the real Joe?" Brian asked.

Jodi suddenly felt dizzy and she sank down on a big rock.

"I know. Oh, poor Joe! Those bad guys must have kidnapped him—just as he feared they would!"

Brian pulled on her arm. "C'mon, Jodi, this is no time to rest! Where would they be holding him?"

"Of course!" Jodi cried, leaping up from the rock. "It's perfect! That old cabin where I saw the face! That's why I saw the message in the dirt for help." She glanced around.

"Hey, look! We've been walking toward the cabin! We're almost there. It should be just around this point of land!"

MaryAnn grabbed Jodi's arm. "No way! I'm not going to that cabin!"

"C'mon, MaryAnn," Jodi said and shook off her hand. "We can't stand here arguing. Joe's life may be at stake. You can go back if you want to, but I'm going to that cabin!"

She whirled around and began running down the beach, swinging her purse and jumping over logs and rocks. Brian and MaryAnn followed more slowly.

They rounded the point of land and now could see one of the windows in the cabin. There was no beach on that side of the point, so they were forced to wade in the water. MaryAnn found it difficult to keep up.

She paused to blow her nose. "Hey, you guys! Wait up!"

Jodi turned back and motioned for her to hurry. "We're almost there," she called back. "Come on!"

Jodi continued jumping from rock to rock and splashing through the shallow water. She had slung her purse around her neck to keep it dry.

The beach widened out and soon Jodi paused in some bushes just below the cabin.

"Now, we have to make *sure* the gang isn't here," she whispered. "Brian, you circle up through these woods to the back of the cabin and see if there's a truck or car there. Also listen quietly at the backdoor and see if you can hear anyone talking. OK?"

Brian saluted. "Right, sarge! Be back on the double!"

"Oh, this is great," MaryAnn grumbled from a log. "Getting my feet wet when I have a cold. And it's raining again. My mother would shoot me!"

Jodi chuckled. "I don't think so, MaryAnn. Just think about poor Joe, being held captive all these days!"

"But why didn't he hear us when we were here before?" MaryAnn asked.

Jodi sat down beside her. "We were really quiet, remember? And the wind was blowing that day—I sure wish it would stop raining. Maybe it will stop." She glanced up at the gray sky.

A little later she heard the bushes crackling and stood up. Brian was running toward them.

"That was fast," Jodi commented.

Brian was panting. "Nobody here—no sounds from the cabin. Hope you're—right about Joe being here!"

Jodi took a deep breath and looked at MaryAnn and Brian.

"I'll leave my purse by this big rock," she said, motioning to a big rock not far away on the beach. "Don't let me forget it! Now, let's go!"

She led the way out into the open beach and studied the cabin. It was built on the side of the hill, so there were two windows high off the ground facing the lake. One of them was boarded up.

They climbed up behind the cabin and listened at the back door.

"Doesn't sound like anyone's here," Jodi said out loud. "I hope the crooks aren't just taking a nap in there!" She took another big breath. "Well, here goes!" With her fist she beat on the door.

"Joe! Joe! Are you in there?" She called and hit the door again. She listened. Nothing. She moved around the wall and beat on the side of the cabin. Brian and MaryAnn followed.

"Joe! It's Jodi! Are you in there?" She listened. Brian looked up suddenly.

"I heard something—" He paused. "There it is again! It sounds like someone pounding, a long way off!"

Jodi snapped her fingers. "He must be on the other side of the cabin—around by the beach. Come on!" She dashed around the cabin.

"Listen!" MaryAnn said suddenly. "You can hear the pounding better over here!" They all looked up at the window.

Jodi waved her hands. "All right. We know Joe is in there. Now we need to figure out a way into the cabin!"

They circled the cabin, searching for a way in. All the windows were boarded up. Suddenly Jodi stopped by the side of the cabin.

"Hey! There's a tiny window up there," she exclaimed, pointing to a small window above their heads. "It isn't boarded up, but I wonder if Brian could squeeze through it."

"I could try!" Brian said. "Here! Give me a boost. I hope the window is unlocked." He took off his shoes and put one foot on Jodi's shoulder and one foot on MaryAnn's shoulder.

The two girls slowly stood up. Brian pounded at the latch on the window.

"It's stuck," he said. "Hey! Don't wiggle!" He steadied himself and gave another blow to the window. Suddenly the latch gave way and the window screeched open. He stuck his head in, grabbed something and disappeared inside.

"Now, go around to the backdoor," Jodi instructed. She and MaryAnn ran to the backdoor. Her heart pounded heavily as they waited. Would Brian be captured, too? Suddenly the doorknob turned and the door swung open. Brian was standing in the semi-darkness of the old cabin.

"Hurry!" he whispered. "Let's find Joe and get out of here!"

Jodi stepped down the dark, moldy-smelling hallway and paused. Her hands were cold and her knees shook. Brian brushed past her and went into a larger room. Jodi and MaryAnn followed. There was a crude table in the center of the room.

"Looks like someone's been eating here," Jodi said. There were used paper plates, tin cans of food, and cigarette stubs lying on the table.

Just then they heard pounding coming from a closed door off the kitchen.

"Joe's in there!" Brian exclaimed. "Come on!" He led the way to the door and opened it. Jodi came behind him. The smell in the room made her gasp.

On a moldy mattress in the corner of the room, sat Joe, bareheaded. His hair was uncombed and his clothing rumpled and dirty. He was tied, and chained to an iron ring embedded in the wall.

He looked up and smiled. "So! You found me! You shore are an answer to my prayers, kids." He dropped his head a bit. "Sorry I look so bad, but that's the way they left me. Chained like a dog. Now, you be a good boy and git that there key in the window." He pointed to a small key standing in the window.

Brian went and got it and unlocked the padlock on his leg.

"They teased me by putting it in that window," Joe said. "Now, untie my hands. Oh! That feels good!" He rubbed his sore wrists and then stood up slowly.

Jodi and MaryAnn stepped to his side. "Come on, Joe," MaryAnn said softly. "Let's get you out of here!" They helped Joe walk across to the door and into the kitchen where he sank down on a chair.

"Oh, I'm dizzy," he said and shook his head. "First time I've been on my feet for two days. At first they were pretty good and let me exercise some. But they been gone an awful lot recently."

"Who are they?" MaryAnn asked.

Jodi nodded. "Yeah. And why did they do this to you?"

Brian waved his hand. "Ask him later! We should get out of here!" He glanced uneasily toward the back-door.

"Boy's right," Joe said as he slowly got to his feet. "Mighty dangerous place to be in right now if those fellars come back. Now, you girls help me down to the beach and I'll tell you where they hid that there boat. We'll make our getaway in that." He chuckled a bit and the color was returning to his cheeks.

At the beach, Joe rested on the big rock and pointed to an old, dead tree down the beach about one hundred feet.

"See that there old tree?" he said. "I heard 'em talkin', and that boat is right in front of the tree, under some bushes. Don't know if you kids can git it—"

Before he finished talking, Jodi grabbed her purse,

turned, and ran toward the old, dead tree. Brian and MaryAnn ran behind her. In a short time, they uncovered the green boat and hauled it out onto the beach. Brian carried the motor and lifted it up onto the boat. Soon the boat was in the water and they were ready to go. Jodi started the motor and turned the boat down the beach.

"Hey, where's Joe?" MaryAnn cried out. The beach was empty!

"Oh, look! There he is!" Brian pointed. "In the lake."

Joe was swimming toward them. Jodi cut the power and Joe clambered into the boat.

He chuckled and wiped the water from his eyes. "Sorry—about that—couldn't resist a dip. Oh, it feels so good!" He paused as Jodi pushed the throttle open. "Now, Jodi! Take her down to the Green Haven. I'll pick up my car, OK?"

Jodi nodded and turned the boat down the lake. Raindrops splashed into her face and the cool air made her shiver. As soon as they had rounded a point of land, she cut the motor to a quiet putter.

"Before we go on," she said to Joe, "I'd really like some questions answered. We're fairly safe here. Now, would you mind starting at the beginning and telling us the whole story?"

Joe nodded and smiled. "Be glad to, kids. After what you've done for me. Course, I don't think it will do any good—"

He paused and gazed out over the treetops. Jodi wanted him to hurry, but she knew she must let him tell it his own way.

"Ya see, my pappy, he was a funny one. Always playing jokes on people, liked to see 'em *work* for what they got. Never did like to just give things away. Not even to me. Well, in his will there was a funny clause. It said that he had found the mother lode but had never been able to work it—" He paused and glanced at Brian.

"Oh, the mother lode is a vein of pure gold below the surface of the ground. The gold nuggets that were first found along the banks of the creeks were washed away from the mother lode. So every miner wants to find the mother lode. That's what Billy Barker did when he opened this whole area up."

Jodi snapped her fingers. "Mother *L,* MaryAnn! On the bottom of the paper! It must mean the mother lode!" She glanced at Joe. "Oh, I'll explain in a minute. So, your father was too old to work the mother lode he had found?"

"Old and sick," Joe replied. "But in the will he never said just where it was. He gave a hint, and I've been lookin' in the dry Williams Creek bed ever since. I didn't really have much hope of findin' it until I came across that letter from Pappy the other day, sayin' something about the silver box."

"And you thought maybe there was a clue in the box," Brian put in. "But what about these bad guys? Who are they?"

Joe put his hand in the air. "I'm acomin' to that, youngun. Well, now, let's see. I gotta tell you about my family. My mother was a beautiful woman, and very brave, so she followed my father when he came for the gold up here. This here country was no place for womenfolk back then. Pneumonia finally got her and she died up here. Pappy buried her down by the crick. It kinda got to him, so he and I left Barkerville for awhile. He married again and had three more children by my stepmother." He sighed.

"Well, my stepbrother Rufus and I never did git along. He was always a rascal, and still is. It's him that is atryin' to keep me from gittin' my inheritance. You see, my pappy said that if I didn't find the mother lode by the time I was sixty-eight, it would go to the next one in line. And that's Rufus." He cleared his throat.

"You see, Jodi," he continued, "I knew Rufus was on my trail that day you went up into the attic. When he

94

and his friends came to the cabin, I didn't want them knowing what we were up to."

"Oh, I see." Jodi nodded. "That's why you took down the ladder."

Joe shook his head. "That rascal! He forced me to go down to my camp by the river and to show him where I'd been diggin'. Later I got away from him, but he grabbed me again, and was pretendin' to be me so you'd give him the box. I tried to write a word in the dirt for help, and I threw my hat overboard so someone would find it." He sighed heavily.

"I saw it, Joe!" Jodi exclaimed. "And we found your hat, too. In a way, it helped us find you! Now I have something to show you." She leaned over, picked up her purse from the bottom of the boat and took out her Bible. Turning it to the yellowed paper in the back, she handed it to Joe.

He looked at it for a long moment and then glanced up, his blue eyes sparkling. "You found this in the silver box!" he said in a hushed voice.

Jodi smiled and nodded. "We took it to a Chinese man and he translated it for us. Those words at the bottom are the meanings of the symbols that are underlined."

"Whoopee!" Joe yelled. "Mother *L*. That means this is the clue to find the mother lode! Whoopee!"

MaryAnn laughed. "That's great, Joe, but I think we'd better be getting on over to the Green Haven before those men find out you're gone. Your car would be the first place they'd check to find you."

Jodi nodded. "You're right. Let's go!" She jammed the throttle over, and the boat leaped through the water. Soon they rounded a point of land and pulled up to the dock of the Green Haven Resort.

MaryAnn glanced around nervously. "I don't like this place," she said.

"C'mon, MaryAnn," Brian urged. "We're with you now. Doesn't look like anyone's around, anyway."

Jodi tied the boat to the pier and glanced toward the office. Had she only imagined it, or had she seen some-one duck behind the corner of the building? She shivered. Then she led the way to Joe's car in the bushes. He lifted the hood and pulled out a key that was wired underneath.

"Always keep this one," he said with a big smile as he opened the door and sat down. "Never know when you might need it. Now, you kids pile in. I'm goin' back to Barkerville, and I'll need help in figurin' out these clues."

Jodi glanced at MaryAnn.

"It won't take long, I promise!" Joe exclaimed. "Why, I'll have you back before your parents even know you're gone!"

"OK!" Jodi replied. "If we hurry. I'd hate to leave you now, with this mystery only half solved." She climbed in and motioned for MaryAnn and Brian.

"Jodi," MaryAnn began. "You know we shouldn't—" She waved her hand. "Hurry! We'll be back soon." They jumped in and Joe started the motor.

"Feel like my old self!" Joe laughed as they swung out onto the road. He pressed the gas pedal down and the little car flew around the corners. Jodi grabbed the edge of the seat and gritted her teeth. They swept past the driveway going into the Bowron Lakes Resort and she could not help looking back. Fear and disapproval were written on MaryAnn's face.

Suddenly a truck barreled around the corner directly toward them! Joe hit the brakes and swerved into the ditch. Then he stepped on the gas, and the car roared up and out.

Jodi glanced at Joe. His face was white. A few sec-onds later he let out a long breath.

"Whew! That was close," he said. "And what's worse, that was Rufus! And I'm sure he recognized me!" He stepped on the gas.

"But—but, Joe!" Jodi exclaimed, grabbing the arm-rest. "You can't go any faster—we'll crash!"

10

Angel's Nose

Joe stared straight ahead, his jaw set stubbornly. He kept the gas pedal down, and the little car skidded around the corners and bounced through the mud puddles. The windshield wipers swished water and mud across the windshield, making it difficult to see. Jodi's blue eyes were wide, her knuckles white from gripping the seat. Finally they reached the blacktop road leading to Barkerville.

Joe drew in a big breath and glanced in the rearview mirror.

"Sorry I had to go so fast," he said. "Those fellars will be on my trail. Cain't let them catch me yet."

Jodi smiled weakly. "Well, we're almost there now."

A few minutes later Joe slowed down to drive past the museum and then turned into a service road that went behind the buildings at Barkerville. He drove for a while and then stopped in front of a big barn.

"Jodi, could you go open those doors?" he asked. "I think I'll hide my car inside for awhile. Nobody comes here much, and those sneaky guys with Rufus won't find it here."

Jodi nodded and jumped out. She swung the doors open and watched as Joe parked the car in one of the stalls. MaryAnn brought Jodi's purse, and Joe shut the door behind them.

Joe paused. "Let's see that there paper, Jodi. What was the first word?" It was raining harder, so they stepped under the eaves of the barn.

Jodi dug her Bible out of her purse and opened it to the yellowed paper.

"Hm," Joe murmured. "First word is 'pan.' Now, I wonder what that means?"

"Mr. Fong said it wasn't an ordinary pan," MaryAnn put in.

Joe scratched his head. "A different kind of pan. I don't know what to think."

"Hey, I know!" Brian said. "I bet it means a gold pan!"

Joe slapped his back. "I betcha you're right, boy! A special gold pan. Hm—there was some gold pans that Pappy gave to the museum. He had got 'em offa Billy Barker. I guess that's why the museum wanted 'em. Let's go look at 'em. At least that's the place to start."

They walked around the barn and came out on the main street. The tourists stared at Joe, but he didn't seem to notice. His sharp eyes searched everywhere as they walked along the boardwalk.

"Gotta keep an eye peeled for these rascals," he said quietly. Jodi shivered.

They were just going in the door of the museum when she heard a truck pull up on the parking lot. She glanced back.

"Oh, look!" she said. "I bet that's them!" Joe peered out of the museum door and nodded.

"Yep, it's them, all right." He pulled Jodi back into the museum. "Rufus knows you. You better stay out of sight. Brian, you stand on the steps there and watch where Rufus goes. But don't let on you're watchin'!"

A few minutes later, Brian came in and reported. "They split up. The small guy went behind Barkerville. The other two headed down the main street."

Joe nodded. "OK. We'll just have to keep a coupla steps ahead of them. Let's look at them gold pans, now."

Jodi turned and followed Joe back to the display of gold pans. Her eyes sparkled with the excitement of a real treasure hunt!

At the display, which showed various kinds of mining equipment, Joe picked up a gold pan.

98

"Don't know if this is the one Pappy gave 'em," he mumbled.

Jodi took it from him and looked at it carefully. On the back she could see some faint scratches.

"Look!" she said, pointing to them. "I think this is a word! It's so faint—what does it say?"

Joe took it closer to the light and studied it, his eyes squinting. "Can't quite—make out—what it says," he said.

"It says," a loud voice spoke up at Jodi's elbow, "Do Not Touch!"

Jodi jumped and whirled around. A pretty girl with long blond hair was frowning at Joe.

"Angel!" Jodi exclaimed.

Angel Lewis shifted her gaze to Jodi. "Do you know this man, Jodi?" she asked, still frowning.

"Why—why, yes!" Jodi replied. "This is Sucker Joe. He lives here in Barkerville. It was his father that gave the museum that gold pan!"

Angel's blue eyes lit up at the mention of Joe's name.

"So, that's his name," she exclaimed. "I heard about him, and that you were working on some treasure hunt with him. Well, part of my job here at the museum is to guard the artifacts, so I'm asking him again to put that gold pan down!"

Joe shifted his feet and cleared his throat. "Well, now, you wouldn't mind if I just looked at this here gold pan, for old times' sake?"

Angel's face softened. "For just a minute—*if* you'll tell me what you're looking for." She smiled coaxingly.

Jodi had been studying the pan in Joe's hand intently. Now she flashed an angry look at the slim girl.

"We won't tell you anything!" she said, her cheeks hot and her head whirling. She glanced at Joe. "You can put that down, Joe. Let's leave—it's *stuffy* in here!"

They paused on the steps of the museum.

"What—what nerve!" Jodi sputtered. "How did she find out so much? I bet she's a spy for Rufus!"

"Jodi," MaryAnn said. "You know you should love her. I think she could be nice!"

Jodi's face turned red. "You would! I suppose you think she's pretty, too! Well, I don't! I think her nose ruins her whole face!"

"Her nose?" Brian asked. "I didn't notice anything wrong with it."

Jodi shook her head. "It's too long!" she spit out. "And she puts it into other people's business!"

MaryAnn chuckled. "Oh, Jodi. You're just jealous because you saw her with Ron the other day."

Joe cleared his throat. "Shore wish I knew what to do next," he said. "Did you see a word scratched on the back of that pan, Jodi?"

"Yes, I did!" Jodi exclaimed, the sparkle returning to her eyes. "But I don't know what it means. The word was *cane.*"

"Cane," Joe mused. "Only thing I ken think of is the cane Pappy used to use all the time—always hung it on a nail in the cabin, and it's still there—"

Brian reached for Jodi's purse. "But that doesn't tell us much. What was the other clue, sis? Maybe that will give us an idea of what to do."

Jodi opened her Bible and looked at the paper. "The other word is temple—church," she said. "Let's go over there! Maybe there's a clue there that will tie everything together!" She heard a noise behind her and turned to see the door close and a flash of blond hair whirl away. Had Angel been listening to their conversation? Would she tell Rufus? She clenched her hands.

Joe glanced around. "Brian, you can be our scout," he said. "You run ahead and see if them fellars are around."

In a few minutes he returned, panting hard. "No sign of 'em, chief!" he said with a grin.

Joe laughed. "OK, heap big brave! Let's go!"

The church was a tall, wooden building with stained glass windows and beautifully polished seats. Jodi sat down in the back pew and sighed.

"Oh, I like this place. It's like an oasis in the desert." She ran her fingers through her wet, curly, red brown hair.

Joe nodded. "A shelter in the time of storm," he said quietly. "Used to sing that old song in here. In the old days, this was the only place you could git away from the hell out there."

"Well, we better start looking," Jodi said, standing up.

MaryAnn wrinkled her nose and sneezed. "What are we looking for?" she asked, glancing around the small building.

"Some word, or clue, scratched or written somewhere in here," Jodi replied. She began searching the doors, doorways, and walls. Brian, MaryAnn, and Joe inspected the pews.

A little later, they all straightened up and looked around when the door squeaked open. An older woman and man with two small children entered. They stared for a moment at Jodi and the others, walked around the building, and then left.

Brian turned to Jodi. "This is crazy," he complained. "There isn't anything scratched or written in here!"

"There *has* to be," Jodi replied. "We just have to keep looking!" At that moment MaryAnn opened a door at the front of the sanctuary that led into a small room.

"Hey!" she said. "This room is lined with old newspapers! Maybe the clue is in here somewhere!" They all crowded into the small room. Jodi's heart beat loudly as she glanced at the newspapers on the wall. Was the secret of the treasure somewhere in this room?

"There are four walls, and there's four of us," she said. "Let's each take a wall. Start at the top and study each paper. Look for a word or words that are underlined or circled."

All was quiet as they studied the papers on the wall.

101

Several people came into the room, glanced around, and then left. Jodi's hopes were beginning to falter when Joe let out a whoop.

"Here's somethin' about Pappy!" he said. "Lookee here. Never knew they put that in the paper. But I don't see anythin' circled."

Jodi, Brian, and MaryAnn crowded close to Joe. The article was a small one, barely ten lines long. Quickly she read it, searching for the circled word. The article told of the strike Joe's father and uncle had made near Williams Creek and the kind of equipment they used.

Jodi's finger slid down the paper. "It says they used a sluicer box," she said and stopped. "Look! Box is circled! The ink is just so faded, it's hard to see!" Joe let out a whoop.

"Does the word *box* mean anything to you?" Jodi asked him as they straightened up.

"Box. Shore! Just below where he always hung his cane is a woodbox. It was kind of fancily carved. Come on! Somethin' must be in that box!"

Suddenly they heard the church door squeak. Jodi scrambled for the door of the small room. No one was in the church. She ran to the outer door, opened it, and glanced around. People streamed by the church in raincoats and carrying umbrellas, but there was no sign of Rufus or his friends.

"Coast is clear," Jodi said to the others. "Now let's get to the cabin!" They stepped out into the rain and hurried along the main street, dodging into the stores, the hairdressers, the livery. Jodi shivered as the rain soaked through her sweater.

"Brr!" Joe exclaimed, mopping his forehead. "Wish I had my hat! At least there's no sign of them crooks!"

Jodi nodded grimly. "I wish we could see them somewhere. It gives me the creeps to have them disappear just like that!" She glanced back and shivered again.

"I hope we can hurry and find the map or whatever

it is," MaryAnn commented between sneezes. "I want to get home!"

Just as they turned the corner that opened into the clearing, Jodi thought she saw a movement in the woods beyond the cabin. She stopped and blinked her eyes. Was it something else? Had she just imagined it? An uneasy, spooky feeling crawled up her back.

Joe motioned for them to be quiet while he circled the cabin and peered into the windows. He returned in a few minutes.

"No sign of 'em here," he said. They trooped inside the cabin and Jodi was surprised it was so clean. She could not help hugging herself from the cold.

Joe stuffed some wood into the wood cookstove. "I'll have a fire going here in a few minutes to take the chill off. Then we'll tackle that woodbox."

Jodi stepped over to the wall and looked at the carved lid of the woodbox. Joe got the fire going, then he lifted the lid. It was empty, except for a few wood chips.

"Seems Pappy built this here box funny," Joe muttered. "I remember he took special pains with the bottom. Now, I wonder why." He lifted the heavy box on its side and inspected the bottom.

Jodi glanced out the window nervously. How soon would it be before Rufus would come to the cabin? MaryAnn stood hunched over the stove, trying to get warm.

Joe had begun tearing the bottom out of the box.

"Yep. Just as I figured!" he said finally. "This box has got a false bottom. In just a minute—" He paused, glancing out the window.

Very slowly he rose to his feet and tiptoed to the door. Jodi, MaryAnn, and Brian stood frozen with fear. Quietly Joe opened the door and stepped out onto the porch. One of the boards squeaked as he stepped on it. There was a rustle under one window. Jodi stared at the window, unable to move.

Joe came back into the cabin. "Musta been a squirrel. We have to be careful, though. Here, I'll git my rifle down and lay it on the table." He took his powerful rifle down from some pegs on the wall, loaded it, and laid it on the table.

Jodi eyed it uncomfortably. "Let's hurry! I want to see what's in that woodbox!"

Joe nodded and went back to work. In a short time he showed Jodi and the others the hidden compartment in the bottom of the box.

"There's something in there!" Jodi said excitedly. "It looks like a tin box!"

"Shore does," Joe muttered. He reached in and drew out a large tin box. Very carefully, as if he were handling dynamite, he laid it on the table.

"I wonder what's in it!" Brian exclaimed. He was nearly dancing with excitement. "It looks heavy. I wonder if it's gold nuggets or something!"

They crowded close as Joe slowly lifted the lid. When it was off, they all stared silently at the contents.

MaryAnn spoke first. "A Bible?" she asked. "I—I thought it would be something—to do with the gold."

Joe lifted the Bible tenderly from the box. It was a very old and large family Bible. Jodi glanced at him and was surprised to see tears in his eyes.

He sat down in a chair and laid the Bible carefully on his lap.

"Well, it may not be what we were expecting," he said slowly and quietly. "But it *is* a treasure."

He looked down at it and stroked its tattered cover. "Yup. Means more to me than all the gold in the world. Ya see, it belonged to my mother. In fact, it was her prized possession. I ken still see her sittin' my the winder here, lettin' the light fall on its pages while she read it." He sighed and wiped his eyes.

Jodi sat down in another chair and sighed, too. "Well, where does that leave us?" she asked.

Joe chuckled and replaced the Bible on the table. "Up a crick, I reckon. Don't know what to do now."

MaryAnn dabbed at her nose with a Kleenex and paced nervously to the door. "Maybe we should go home, Jodi," she said. "We can work on this tomorrow."

Jodi stood up. "But, MaryAnn! We can't! We're going home tomorrow, remember?" She stiffened and glanced toward the door. A board had screeched on the porch. Joe reached for his gun.

But suddenly the door flew open. Rufus was standing there with a rifle pointed at Joe!

11

Getting It Right

"I wouldn't touch that gun, Joe," he said slowly. "Now, git away from it! All of you! Over to that wall!" He waved the gun toward the far wall.

Jodi's heart was pounding in her ears and her knees were shaking like leaves. She seemed rooted to the spot. Joe slowly stood up. His shoulders sagged.

"C'mon, kids," he said sadly. "He means business. He'd shoot his own mother!" They walked to the far wall and stared at Rufus.

"Enough out of you, old man!" Rufus shouted. He stepped into the cabin, followed by a short, dark man, and a fat-bellied bearded man.

Jodi swallowed hard and glanced at MaryAnn. Her face was white and her brown eyes were staring wide at the gun pointed at them. Brian moistened his lips and glanced at Jodi. She laid her hand on his shoulder.

Rufus inspected the woodbox, glanced at the Bible, and then made a quick survey of the rest of the cabin. Then he turned to Joe.

"All right. Where is it?" he asked with a sneer. "Thought you could hide it, huh? Well, I'll git it anyway. Now, talk!"

Joe chuckled. "What are you looking for, Rufus? A box of gold nuggets? You know as well as I do that Pappy never mined that mother lode."

Rufus strode over to Joe and pointed the gun at his stomach. "But you found something, Joe!" he screamed. "You followed them clues and you found something! I know cuz if you hadn't found it, you'd still be lookin'! Now, where's the map, or instructions, or whatever that'll tell me where that mother lode is!"

Joe shook his head sadly. "We didn't find nothin',

Rufus. All we found is mother's old family Bible. Maybe it was just a joke and there was no gold vein. You know how Pappy loved a good joke!"

Rufus stared at him, silent for a moment or two. Then he backed away, his gun still pointed toward Joe and the others.

"Find some rope!" he barked at his buddies. They began searching through the cabin and outside.

Big Red, who had called himself "Alan Young," returned first. "Ain't none," he said.

Just then Shorty returned with an old rope looped over his arm.

"Found some down by that old barn," he said. "Want me to tie 'em up, boss?"

Rufus sneered. "That's the idea, Shorty. Maybe they'll git their memory back after they've been hogtied for awhile." He paused and scratched his head. "Maybe I'll try gittin some ransom money offen that dark-headed one. Hear her dad's in the dough!"

Shorty had them sit down on the floor while he tied their legs and hands together. Jodi gasped as the man pulled the rope tight and it cut into her ankles and wrists. There was no hope of wiggling free.

She leaned against the wall and glanced at MaryAnn. She could see one tear trickling down her white face and her slim shoulders were bowed forward. Jodi moved until her arm brushed against MaryAnn.

"Hey!" Jodi whispered softly. "We'll get out of here. The Lord will help us. Hasn't He promised?"

MaryAnn shook her head. "Oh, Jodi! I'm so afraid! What are we going to do?"

Rufus glanced in their direction. "Shut up, you kids. There'll be no talkin'."

Jodi nudged MaryAnn. "Pray!" she whispered.

Joe cleared his throat and straightened up. "Lookee here, Rufus," he said in a congenial tone of voice. "Holdin' me, that's OK. I'm kin. I may not even press charges. But holdin' these kids is somethin' else. Do you

107

know how many years you'd git for kidnappin'? And all for a vein of gold that we don't know for sure is there? If I was you, I'd let these here kids go."

Rufus stalked over to Joe and jabbed him with his toe.

"But you ain't me and that makes a lot of difference," he said. "I'm just countin' on one of these kids losin' their nerve and spillin' the whole kettle of beans right in my lap!" He put his head back and laughed loudly.

He stopped suddenly and whirled to Jodi. She cringed back.

"Now, here's the girl, that's been buckin' me all along." He grabbed her shoulder. "Now, you tell me, girlie, all about those clues and what you found here in the cabin!" He shook her.

"Take your hands off her!" Joe yelled.

Rufus laughed and straightened up. "Oh, so you're gittin' bossy, huh? Well, suppose you tell me or I'll rough up these kids some!"

"I been tellin' you!" Joe shouted angrily. "There ain't no paper or map! All's we found is that Bible!"

Rufus thudded across the cabin and turned to his men. "All right, men. Let's search this cabin. I'm goin' to start with the young lady's purse!" He dumped out Jodi's purse and rifled the contents.

He picked up the Bible and then tossed it back onto the table. It fell open to the maps and the yellowed paper. He grabbed it up and studied it.

"Oh, ho!" he exclaimed. "So this is what you found in the silver box! Pretty nifty hiding place." He looked at it again and then glanced up. "The clue in the church led you to the woodbox. And you found something else besides that there Bible!"

Rufus and the two men tore the cabin apart, searching for a map. It was getting dark outside and Jodi's arms ached. Brian leaned over on her shoulder and took a little nap.

A little later, he woke up and leaned against the wall.

"Hungry!" he whispered to Jodi.

She nodded. Her stomach was growling, too. Suddenly tears came to her eyes as she thought of her mother and father and the agony they must be going through. All because of her! Why, oh, why had she not stopped and told them where she was going? Why had she not phoned the police from the Green Haven?

"Dumb-head!" she whispered to herself and sniffed.

Rufus settled down in a chair. "Well, we haven't found a thing. Musta hid that map somewhere really good." He yawned. "Well, I got lots of time, and it don't look like they're going nowhere!"

Shorty and Big Red laughed with Rufus. Then Rufus stood up and walked over to Joe.

"Gittin' hungry?" he asked.

Joe nodded and glanced up. "You might say that. These here kids'll be gittin' hungry, too."

Rufus smiled wickedly. "Probably thirsty, too. For a nice, cool drink of water."

Jodi had not noticed before, but now that he mentioned it, she realized she was dying for a drink. She wet her lips with her tongue and her mouth felt dry.

Rufus knelt down and spoke confidentially. "Listen here. I got grub and water, too. I'll be glad to share it. Of course, for a price. Let's say the information I want will buy you supper and a big drink of water and your freedom. How about it?" He poked Brian with his finger.

Brian drew back and shook his head. "There isn't any map!" He put his head back and his lips quivered.

Rufus shook his head. "Real willpower. Never seen anything like it." He stood up. "All right. When you're ready for your dinner and some water, you just tell me. Otherwise, you're goin' to git mighty hungry!"

Jodi heard a sniff and turned to look at MaryAnn. MaryAnn shook her head.

"It's no use, Jodi," she whispered. "It'll be a long time before anyone figures out where we are!"

Jodi shook her head. "Mom and Dad knew I was

helping Joe. The police know where Joe lives. They will be here soon, MaryAnn. I'm sure of it!"

"I hope you're right! Rufus would let us starve!" MaryAnn leaned back against the wall and closed her eyes.

Rufus added some wood to the fire in the woodstove and started preparing his own supper. Soon he and his friends were sitting down to eat. The warm smell of food nearly drove Jodi crazy. She kept swallowing saliva, remembering her meager lunch. She wished she had eaten more!

She glanced at Brian. "You OK?" she whispered.

He sniffed and then tried to smile. "Sure. You think the police will come soon?" Tears glistened in his eyes.

Jodi nodded. "I'm sure of it. Just keep holding on!"

Rufus leaned back in his chair. "Been thinkin' the cops are going to be on our trail purty soon," he said to Big Red. "We'd better move outa here. They know enough to check out Joe's cabin."

"Down to the camp?" Big Red asked.

Rufus nodded. "Let's go!" He slammed down his chair and stood up. Shorty untied the ropes on their hands and feet and they stood up.

"Where—where are you taking us?" Brian asked shakily.

Rufus laughed. "Where you won't be found, kid." He picked up his gun and Joe's rifle, and herded them out the door. The rain had let up and the air was fresh.

Jodi breathed deeply of the cool air. It felt good to be outside again and moving around. But her hopes of the police's finding them were dashed. Discouraged, hungry, and tired, she stumbled behind Joe, wiping away the tears that kept coursing down her cheeks.

Rufus led them to the dry creek bed, and they tripped over rocks and logs as they followed him down the creek to his camp. Soon he stopped in front of two tents.

"Put 'em in your tent," he said to Shorty. "You guys

110

can sit outside and keep guard." Shorty pushed them into a tent and had them sit on the floor. Then they tied their hands and feet again.

Jodi looked gratefully at the sleeping bag on the floor of the tent and the can of mosquito repellent. Already the mosquitoes were buzzing around their heads and landing on any exposed skin.

Jodi rolled to the can and grasped it with her hands. Then she rolled back and squirted some of the repellent on each of the others. MaryAnn then took the can and squirted some on her.

"Whew!" Jodi said, blinking her eyes. "There's enough of that stuff in this tent to kill the mosquitoes, plus us!"

"What's our chances of getting out of here?" Brian asked Joe.

Joe shook his head. "Mighty slim. Them two guys Rufus has with him are tough. Been in and out of prison most of their lives. Our only hope is someone finding us."

MaryAnn shook her head. "If we'd only let someone know where we were going!" She sniffed and glanced at Jodi. Then she turned quickly away.

"I—I guess it's my fault," Jodi said slowly, the tears welling up in her eyes again. She sighed. "I can't do anything right, can I?" She leaned against Joe's shoulder and sobbed.

"Now, that's no way to carry on," Joe said. "If it's anyone's fault, it's mine. But it don't help none to cry about it and blame each other. Let's just watch for a chance to git away. It may be they'll get careless. And you can bet your bottom dollar we'll only get one chance!"

Brian nodded. "I just remembered about Paul and Silas in jail. They were a whole lot worse off than we are. But they sang in the middle of the night. So let's sing! Come on, Jodi, you start something!"

111

Jodi smiled a little through her tears. "OK, I guess if Paul and Silas can, we can, too. But first I need a Kleenex. Does anyone have one?"

MaryAnn nodded. "Yeah. A used one, in my front jeans' pocket, but I can't get it. Maybe if you moved over here with your back to me, you could get it out."

Jodi squirmed around, dug out the Kleenex and then had to ask MaryAnn to wipe her nose. Suddenly Mary-Ann began giggling and Jodi laughed, too. Then they sang several choruses.

Suddenly the tent flap flew open. "Cut out the singin'," Rufus growled and let the tent flap fall down again.

It was quiet in the tent for a few minutes. Joe rolled to his side and peered out the tent door.

Jodi's heart was heavy. She knew she had made the wrong decision and they were all paying the consequences. Soon she lay down in a tight circle and managed to pull some of the sleeping bag over her.

Joe turned from the tent door. "God must be with us!" he whispered. "They're breakin' out the booze. Maybe they'll get so drunk they'll fall asleep and we'll get our chance! We have to keep watch, though." He turned back to the tent door.

Darkness had fallen and the cold seeped through the thin tent walls. Jodi, MaryAnn, and Brian huddled close together and shared the sleeping bag. Soon Jodi could hear regular breathing from MaryAnn and Brian.

But sleep would not come to her. The men outside were loud. A heavy blanket of guilt and discouragement weighed her down. She could see her frantic, concerned parents praying through the night. She went over and over in her mind those things she had done wrong. Finally she opened her eyes in the darkness.

She looked over toward Joe. He had moved away from the tent door and was cuddled up next to Brian, his heavy breathing revealing that he was asleep.

Jodi sighed. *Oh, God, I don't know why you bother*

with me. I'm no good for anything. Look at the mess I've made out of this! She paused.

Suddenly a scene came back to her. It was so real she could almost reach out and touch it. There were Mrs. Christy and herself, sitting beside the lake. All was quiet. Mrs. Christy smiled and began speaking. What was it she had told her that day?

The words came back to her in the darkness of the tent.

"Did you know God designed you just as you are? Do you question the Master Artist on His design? . . . 'for I am fearfully and wonderfully made' . . . 'thank You for making me' . . . We should ask God to forgive us for being bitter, and we should thank Him for even the things we don't like about ourselves . . . He isn't finished with you yet, Jodi, or me either."

Jodi swallowed and her eyes moistened with tears. She knew God was with her here in this tent. He had reminded her of Mrs. Christy's wise counsel. She batted her long lashes and gazed into the darkness.

*Oh, Lord, forgive me for being bitter about the way you made me, and for disobeying Dad and not telling him where we were going. Thank You for making me just the way You did—big nose and all. And—and I want to thank You for letting this happen to me. I really need Your help—*She paused. *And—and I do accept myself just as I am. Help me to live for You and never to run myself down again. Thank You so much!*

She closed her eyes and a smile rested lightly on her lips. Suddenly her eyes flew open again.

Oh, yes. I forgot, Lord. Please help get us out of this mess! She snuggled down closer to MaryAnn and drifted off to sleep.

12

Jodi's Folly

Jodi blinked open her eyes. Had she been asleep? Joe, MaryAnn, and Brian were still sleeping. It was dark outside, but the darkness was lifting and she sensed it was early morning. The camp was quiet.

Very slowly she rolled away from the pile of sleeping bodies. MaryAnn muttered something in her sleep, readjusted herself, and went back to sleep. Brian opened his eyes. Jodi moved so she could whisper in his ear.

"Be still. I'm going to try to see if those men are asleep. This may be our chance."

Brian nodded. "Jodi!" he whispered. "I've been working on my ropes. I think I have one hand loose. Here, move over by me so I can feel your ropes. Maybe I can get them undone."

Carefully Jodi rolled her back close to Brian's back. She could feel his hand trying to loosen the ropes. He worked for some time and then grunted and relaxed.

"No, I can't do it," he whispered.

Jodi rolled over. "It's OK. I'm going to look outside." She rolled to the door of the tent and peered out. A thin streak of light glimmered in the east. She could see the other tent and where the fire had been. But she could not see any of the men.

She wiggled until she had her head out the door. Only a few feet away lay Big Red, partially propped up against a log, sound asleep. His rifle lay across his lap and there were several bottles strewn in the grass around him.

Moving slowly and deliberately, she rolled out the tent door and turned onto her back. Then she sat up. Her heart gave a leap as she spotted, only a few feet away, a hunting knife lying on a rock by the fire.

She glanced at Big Red and at the other tent door.

114

Oh, God, help me now! she prayed silently and lay down on her side. Slowly she rolled through the dirt and rocks to where the knife was. Rolling onto her back, she felt it against her hand, and her fingers closed over the handle.

Suddenly there was a rustle in the grass. She froze. Turning her head, she looked at Big Red. He had moved in his sleep, muttering to himself. He adjusted himself and went back to sleep.

She sighed with relief and rolled over and over until she slipped under the tent door. She turned to Brian.

"I got a knife!" she whispered. "I'll roll to your back. Can you use that one hand and cut my ropes?"

Brian's brown eyes popped wide with excitement. "Just let me at 'em!" he replied.

She wiggled until her back was to his back. "Just don't cut me!" she whispered. She could feel him grasp the knife and begin to saw against the ropes that held her hands. In a few minutes, the ropes loosened and then fell off.

She sat up. "I'm free!" she whispered. She rubbed her sore wrists gently. "Oh, that feels good!" She wiggled her fingers to get the feeling back in them. Then she cut Brian's ropes and the ropes that held her ankles.

Joe rolled over, and his eyes widened. Silently Jodi cut his ropes and then MaryAnn's. Everyone rubbed wrists and ankles until the feeling returned. Joe peered out the tent door.

"Still sleeping," he whispered. "But we have to be careful. Now, here's what we'll do. One by one we'll walk through camp and hide in them bushes over there. Then we'll run to the cabin, grab somethin' to eat and drink, and then git my car." Brian nodded and rubbed his empty stomach.

"OK," Jodi whispered. "Who's first?" Her mouth was dry and there was a whole flock of butterflies assembled in her stomach. She felt just like she did before she performed on her horse Honey at the gymkhana.

"You go first," Joe instructed. "Just go slow and easy. We'll get through." He patted Jodi's arm and held the tent door open for her.

She stuck her head out and looked around. The light in the east was becoming brighter. In a few minutes, Rufus and the others might wake up. Big Red was still asleep.

She crawled out of the tent and stood up. For a second her head spun and her feet wobbled. But then she regained her balance and crept across the camp, choosing her steps as carefully as a cat in a swamp. Soon she reached the first fringe of bushes and stepped behind them. Letting out a sigh of relief, she peered through the bushes. Who was next?

Brian's head appeared over the tent. He moved carefully but quickly. *Too quickly!* Jodi thought. *He'll fall!* But he reached the bushes and knelt down beside Jodi. She smiled at him and he grinned back.

MaryAnn was next, and it seemed to take her an eternity to pick her way across the camp. She stopped every few minutes to choose her next steps. Jodi glanced at the sky. It was getting brighter every second!

"Hurry!" she whispered, her fists clenched tightly at her side. MaryAnn reached the bushes and squatted down. Her face was white but she smiled at Jodi.

They all peered anxiously through the bushes.

"Just Joe," MaryAnn whispered. "He'll make it!"

Jodi could see Joe's head above the tent. She held her breath. Would they really make it away? Joe glanced around and then turned and crept carefully toward them. Suddenly his head disappeared and she could hear a loud *thump,* pans clattering, and Joe's, *"Oof!"*

Joe had fallen! Jodi could see the tent where Rufus and Shorty were sleeping move and could hear grunts coming from it. She and Brian lurched from the bushes and ran to help Joe.

Big Red rolled over and groaned. He lifted his head

116

groggily. Brian and Jodi reached Joe, grabbed his arms, and helped him to his feet. Jodi gasped for breath.

"Hurry!" Brian said. "They're waking up!" Jodi tried to hurry, but everything seemed to move in slow motion.

"Hey!" Big Red muttered, sitting up. "What's goin' on? Hey! Rufus! Shorty!" He grabbed for his gun.

Jodi, Brian, and Joe plowed into the cover of the bushes. MaryAnn had run down the trail, so they did not pause, but continued running. They could hear the men shouting in the camp, and a few minutes later they heard the bushes crackling behind them.

Jodi was the last in line on the narrow trail, but she did not dare look back. At one spot, Joe left the trail and plowed into the thick underbrush of the woods. Jodi leaped over logs and clawed through tangles of bushes. Branches scratched her face, and her side hurt from running.

Panting hard, they finally broke out into the clearing beside the cabin, ran across it, and paused on the porch of the cabin.

Joe's face was red as he paused for breath. "Cain't—git any—food," he said. "They're comin'—come on, follow me. I know a place to hide out." He leaped off the porch.

Jodi could hear the men thrashing in the woods nearby. In a few minutes they would burst out into the clearing. She paused. They really needed food. And there was something else she had to get!

"Just a minute!" she called to Joe and the others who had started off across the clearing. He paused and glanced back.

She dashed into the cabin. On the table was a plastic bag with a loaf of bread in it. She grabbed the bread and then picked up the big, heavy Bible they had found in the woodbox. She ran out the door.

"Hurry!" Brian yelled. "They're getting closer!"

117

She ran across the clearing awkwardly, her body off balance from the heavy Bible. Joe led the way into the woods but shortly stopped and glanced back at Jodi.

"What do you have there?" he asked. "Mother's Bible? Why did you bring that?"

Jodi shook her head. "I just felt like I should," she panted. "Here, Brian, you carry the bread. I can manage the Bible."

MaryAnn frowned at Jodi. "You shouldn't have brought it. It will slow us down," she said.

"It won't slow me down," Jodi replied defensively. "Now, let's get going. Sounds like the men are at the cabin!"

Joe nodded and then turned and led the way deeper into the woods. They climbed over logs and through clumps of underbrush. Jodi's breath came in gasps as she struggled with the heavy Bible. The others, some distance ahead, crawled up a steep hill.

When she reached it, she paused and then took a running start at it, grabbing for a little bush three-fourths of the way up. But the bush pulled out by the roots. Jodi slid and tumbled to the bottom. She lay on her back, the breath knocked out of her for a few seconds.

"Are you all right?" Joe's voice floated down to her from the woods above the hill.

Jodi sat up. In trying to protect the Bible she had skinned her arms and bruised her legs against the rocks. She spit out the dirt from her mouth and nodded.

"Guess so," she called back and stood up, brushing the dirt from her clothes. "I'll try farther down." She went down the gully a little way and climbed the hill where there were more trees and bushes. At the top of the hill she could see a dry creek bed on the other side.

Joe pointed to it. "Used to be a crick joining Sunshine Crick right there," he said. "Both of 'em dried up now. My camp's down around that corner 'bout half a mile."

He began making his way down the hill. "There's an

old cave down here," he said. "Make a dandy place to rest and hide."

Near the bottom of the hill was a large hole in the side of the bank. Joe inspected it and then motioned for the others to follow him in.

Jodi sat on a rock just inside the opening of the hole and sighed. She balanced the Bible on her lap. Mary-Ann sat on another rock farther into the cave, and Brian and Joe sprawled out on the cool, sandy ground.

"Where does it go, Joe?" Brian asked, peering into the darkness.

Joe shook his head. "Just a little ways in there," he said. He glanced up at the low ceiling. "Looks like someone dug this here hole. See those pick marks? Musta been lookin' for gold, gave up, and filled the shaft in with rocks. Big pile of rocks at the back here."

MaryAnn cleared her throat. "I don't know about anyone else, but I'm going to die if I don't get something to drink. Is there water around here, Joe?"

Joe nodded. "Shore is. 'Bout a quarter of a mile." He stood up. "There's an old bucket by the crick, too. It's where I git my water when I'm at the camp. I'll be back. If those guys come around, git way back inside the cave."

To keep her mind off her thirst and hunger, Jodi turned the pages of the Bible. It appeared to have been very well used, with verses underlined and notations made in the margin.

"I wonder if she was a Christian," Jodi said softly.

MaryAnn glanced at her. "Who?"

"Joe's mother," she replied and returned to reading and flipping pages.

A little later, Joe came back with water dripping from an old bucket. Jodi took her turn at the dipper and then sighed.

"Ah," she said. "Nothing tastes better than cold creek water. Especially when you're thirsty!" After

119

their drink, she got out the bread and passed it around. They bowed their heads and thanked God for His protection.

Brian chewed for some time and then glanced at Jodi. "Don't want to complain, but this is a little stale."

MaryAnn grinned. "Yeah. It would taste a lot better with some peanut butter and jelly on it." She paused and considered her piece. "But we should be thankful we have this. Jodi was the only one who dared to go after it."

"But why she ever packed that Bible out here I'll never know." Brian shook his head.

Jodi finished her bread and continued to flip through the pages. "I'll show you, smarty," she said. "I had a reason—a good one!"

She finished the main text and patiently turned through the concordance. Finally she reached the maps in the back.

Suddenly she stopped turning the pages and bent intently over a map.

"Hey! Look at this!" she exclaimed excitedly. She moved out into the sunshine and the others crowded around.

"Look, Joe! This faded writing! Someone has written over the top of the words on this map!" Jodi pointed.

Joe leaned over the map, trying to make out the faint marks written on it. He took the Bible from Jodi and pulled it closer. His finger traced a line and his lips mumbled names. Then he straightened up with a big grin on his face.

"Whoopee!" he shouted. "Whoopee!"

13

God's Forgiveness

"Joe!" Jodi exclaimed and tugged on his sleeve. "Be quiet! Those men—"

Joe nodded. "Oh, yeah. I plum fergot. But, Jodi! Do you know what this is you found here?"

"I think I do." She smiled.

Brian danced around in excitement. "The map for the mother lode! You thought it might be in there, didn't you, Jodi?"

Joe sat down on a rock and began studying the map intently.

"Well, I had this hunch," Jodi replied.

"Hunch!" MaryAnn sniffed. "Cases aren't solved by hunches, Jodi. How many times do I have to tell you that?" MaryAnn smiled and reached her arm around Jodi's shoulders.

"I've been wrong all along," she said softly. "But I got some things right with the Lord last night. I haven't been the friend to you I should have been. Will you forgive me?"

Jodi nodded, her long lashes batting tears away. "Sure, MaryAnn. I settled some things last night, too. I don't want to go around running myself down anymore. I know God made me as I am, and if that's good enough for Him, it's good enough for me!" She hugged Mary-Ann and they laughed together.

Suddenly Joe jumped up and shoved the Bible into Brian's hands.

"Whaddaya know," he said, turning around and gazing for some time at the hole they were sitting in front of. "Whaddaya know."

"What, Joe?" Jodi asked. "What did you find out?"

He took a step or two into the mouth of the cave.

121

"This here old mine shaft! Back in there a ways is the mother lode Pappy found! Right here under my nose all the time!"

"You're kidding!" MaryAnn exclaimed. They all ran into the hole and Brian began throwing rocks to one side. Joe laid his hand on his shoulder.

"No use doin' that, youngun," he said. "It's down a ways, I reckon. Pappy didn't want just anybody findin' it." He glanced around. "This is on my land, too, so there's no hassle about claims. We haven't never sold our mineral rights."

"Do you think it would be safe to go back to Barkerville, now?" Jodi asked. "I'm sure our parents are worried about us."

Joe nodded. "OK. I want to phone my attorney in Vancouver. Tomorrow's my birthday. Then I ken start mining this here gold!" His blue eyes flashed.

He led the way out of the cave, picked up the Bible, and glanced around. "Follow me. I'll take you back to Barkerville through the woods. Don't dare show up on the road."

They threaded their way through bushes, over logs, up and down hills. Joe needed no path to find his way as he knew exactly where he was going. Jodi followed behind him, her stomach growling. Two slices of bread was not enough to fill her up. She was thirsty again, too.

Finally, after it seemed they had hiked for miles and miles, Joe led the way down a hill, and she could see the tops of cars.

"Oh!" MaryAnn exclaimed. "The parking lot! And right over there is the museum. You brought us *around* Barkerville!"

Joe grinned. "Yup. And there's a phone in the museum. We can go there and you kids can phone your parents."

"And the police!" Jodi added as they walked across the parking lot. *What a relief!* she thought. She ran her

122

fingers through her tousled red brown hair and brushed the dirt from her jeans.

Angel Lewis was at the desk in the museum and her deep blue eyes grew wide when they trooped in.

"Could we use the telephone?" Jodi asked crisply. "It's very important."

Angel nodded. "Sure. Where have you been, Jodi? Everyone's looking for you! And you look a sight!"

Jodi moved to the phone and ignored Angel's remark. She looked up the number for the Bowron Lakes Resort and dialed it. After several rings, she hung up.

"No one answered!" she exclaimed. "That seems strange." She turned back and dialed the RCMP detachment in Wells. A secretary answered.

"Hello. This is Jodi Fischer . . . Yes, I'm all right . . . The others are with me . . . I'm at the museum at Barkerville . . . OK. Thanks." She turned to the others.

"She's going to radio some officers to come here. They will also get hold of our parents."

Angel sidled nearer to Jodi. "What *have* you been doing? I'm dying with curiosity, Jodi. Please tell me."

She sniffed. "Well, we got kidnapped by these crooks. And they held us overnight, but we got away this morning. Then we hid out in this cave, and I found a map to a hidden treasure in that old Bible Joe's got!" She glanced at Joe. Joe was frowning and shaking his head. She gulped. Had she said too much?

Suddenly from the hallway leading into the displays, Rufus stepped out, holding a rifle pointed at them! Angel screamed and the others froze. Joe gripped the Bible closer to him.

Rufus grinned wickedly, and Jodi wondered how she had ever confused the two men.

"He, he, he!" he laughed. "I gotcha this time. Now, just give me that there Bible and I'll take you, Joe, and tie you up again. Just till tomorrow this time. Then I git that inheritance, and I'll know where to find it!"

Jodi suddenly felt sick. She glanced at Joe and his face was white. He gripped the Bible tighter and stared at Rufus.

Rufus stepped closer to Joe and punched him in the stomach. "Give it here!" he screamed. "I heard that the police are coming. And I don't think these girls want to see someone shot right in front of them!"

Joe shook his head and his shoulders drooped. Slowly he handed the Bible to Rufus who snatched it up and tucked it under his arm.

"OK, now, march! We're going into hiding and not even these kids will find us this time!" He jabbed Joe again in the stomach and began moving to the door.

Jodi clenched her fists. "He *can't* get away with it!" she muttered. Tears began rolling down her face. "It's all *my* fault! If I wasn't such a—" She stopped suddenly. No! She wouldn't run herself down again, not even now!

Rufus reached the door. "Now, you all stand way back and don't make a move, or I'll shoot the feathers out of old Joe!" He yanked the door open.

Suddenly hands reached around the door and grabbed Rufus! After a brief struggle, someone took his gun. Joe snatched the Bible out of his arms.

Jodi blinked the tears away. A second later she knew who was at the door. Officer Davis! She looked beyond him and saw several other officers! Officer Davis pulled Rufus out of the museum and leaned him against the building. Jodi and the others stepped outside.

Jodi's head whirled and the tears flowed down her cheeks again. She sniffed and MaryAnn handed her a well-used Kleenex. Jodi smiled her thanks and squeezed her arm. Officer Davis stepped up to her.

"How are you?" he asked them.

Jodi smiled. "We're fine now! Boy, am I glad you got here just in time!" Some of the other policemen put handcuffs on Rufus and hurried him to a waiting van. There were two other men in the van.

Officer Davis smiled. "We were right here in Barkerville, looking for you," he said. "I think your parents will be right along, too."

Suddenly an icy cold hand gripped Jodi's arm. She jumped and turned around. Angel's white face loomed up next to hers.

"Oh, I was so afraid, Jodi!" she said. "I—I feel like I'm going to faint!"

MaryAnn took Angel's arm and led her to the top step. "Just sit down here," she said. "Put your head down between your knees." Angel did as she was told, and in a few minutes the color came back to her cheeks.

Officer Davis turned to Jodi. "These are the men we've been looking for. We'll get them on so many charges, they'll be put away for years. Maybe for life, with triple charges of kidnapping against them. We picked up that worker at the Green Haven, too. He was in with these guys." He smiled. "We have you to thank, Jodi. Even though things were a bit rough."

Jodi nodded. "I'll say. I didn't have much hope of getting out. Did you pick those other two up at Joe's cabin?"

Officer Davis nodded. "Yes. Then they let it slip that Rufus was going to try to get you in the museum."

Jodi glanced at Angel. She had stood up and was walking away toward Barkerville. "I wonder where she's going," she said under her breath. "And what she's had to do with this mystery."

In a few minutes Angel returned with packages in her hands. She gave them to Jodi, Brian, MaryAnn, and Joe. Jodi unwrapped hers. It was a chicken sandwich! The others exclaimed over the treat.

Angel blushed. "I heard Brian mention he was hungry so I went and got these at the cafe—I—I really am sorry about messing things up for you, Jodi. Rufus came into the museum several days ago and questioned me about you. He offered to pay me for information and told me about the clues and the gold. I thought it was just a game." She paused, looking down at the ground.

Jodi put her arm around Angel's slender shoulders.

"It's OK, Angel," she said. "I was guilty of a lot of foolish things, too. The important thing is that God can forgive us and that Joe will get his inheritance now!"

Just then the motor home came skidding to a stop in front of the museum. Mr. and Mrs. Fischer, Mr. Laine, and the twins came piling out.

"Jodi! Brian!" Mrs. Fischer called. Jodi and Brian fell into their parents' arms. MaryAnn ran to her father.

"Are you all right?" Mr. Fischer asked. "Looks like Brian is—he's eating, as usual!" He patted Brian's shoulder. Everyone laughed and exchanged stories.

"And, Dad, before you scold me," Jodi said. "I want to say I'm sorry for running off like we did. Believe me, I paid for it!"

Mr. Fischer put his arm around Jodi. "Well, it saddens me to think you couldn't trust me enough to tell me where you were going—but, I do think you've been punished enough." He gazed at her seriously.

A little later Mr. Laine drove the motor home next to a picnic table, and Mrs. Fischer invited Joe and Angel to come for lunch.

Joe smiled. "I shore would be pleased to," he said. "Excuse me, though, while I phone my attorney. If I can use the museum phone, Angel."

Angel nodded. "Sure! And I'll get permission to come over."

After lunch, everyone sat at the picnic table, feeling good.

"Oh, it shore does feel good to be fed up," Joe drawled, patting his full stomach. Everyone laughed.

Mrs. Fischer nodded. "You be sure and stop in sometime on your way through Richburg, Joe. I'm a better cook at home."

Joe grinned. "Thank 'e, Mrs. Fischer. I'll do that." Then he stood up.

"Folks," he said. "I want to say a little piece and then I'll be on my way—I ain't much of a one with

126

words, so I'll make this short and sweet. I was really a down-and-out quitter before Jodi came to see me. I don't know why, but she wanted to help an old geezer like me. Her and MaryAnn helped me to find God's forgiveness fer my sins." He paused, his voice quavering.

"Nobody but God will know how much that meant to me. Then Jodi and Brian and MaryAnn found me and helped solve this mystery. Because of their help, I've found a lost gold mine that my Pappy willed me. I want to say that part of the money I git from the gold mine will go to the Fischers fer their work with the Indian people."

"Joe! That's great!" Mr. Laine exclaimed. His face, usually so serious and closed, was glowing with a big smile. MaryAnn stared at him in amazement.

Joe continued. "I kept tryin' to think of some way to show Jodi and the others how much I appreciated what they've done fer me." He paused and looked around at Heather. "Heather, would you go git that fer me now?" he asked.

Braids flying, the little girl ran to the motor home with Heidi at her heels. Both girls were only gone for a few minutes. They returned with smiles and something held behind their backs.

"I think I finally thought of something. You girls can give that there thing you're hidin' to Jodi," Joe said and sat down.

With twinkles in their eyes, the twins laughingly deposited something heavy in Jodi's hands. Everyone gasped!

"Oh!" Jodi exclaimed, staring at it. "The silver box! Isn't it beautiful!" She held it up for everyone to see. The silver, newly polished, gleamed in the sunlight, and the twin emeralds sparkled. "Are you sure, Joe? This means so much to you!"

Joe grinned. "No, my mind is made up. I want you to have it. Angel found me some silver polish in the museum and my spies here, Heather and Heidi, found the box. Just remember old Joe once in a while!"

Jodi touched the engraved design of the dragon on the lid. "Thank you, Joe," she said, struggling against tears. Suddenly she straightened up and grinned. Her blue eyes sparkled.

"Now I have something for you, Joe!" She sprang up from the table and ran to the motor home, returning with a wide-brimmed felt hat in her hands. With a little bow she handed it to Joe.

"My hat!" Joe cried, his eyes lighting up with pleassure. He folded some creases in it and placed it lovingly on his head. Everyone cheered.

Mr. Laine cleared his throat and stood up. "Well, now," he said. "This seems a time for speeches and I have a little piece to say, too—Joe here was talking about God's forgiveness. I guess I've lived my life thinking I could make it without God. But while we were on this canoe trip, I realized how foolish I was. And— well, it's a long story, but one night I had a little talk with God, and now I know He has forgiven me, too." His voice broke with emotion.

"Oh, Dad!" MaryAnn cried, jumping from her chair and embracing her father. Watching the two, Jodi felt the tears begin to trickle down her cheeks once more. She just knew that soon Mrs. Laine would follow in her husband's steps.

Later Jodi and MaryAnn walked toward Barkerville with Joe to tell him good-bye. On the way back, Jodi squeezed MaryAnn's arm.

"This has been the neatest camping trip ever!" she said, her face shining. "And you know what else?"

MaryAnn looped her arm through Jodi's and shook her dark head. "What?" she asked with a smile.

"Angel really *is* nice!"